Trick
or
Treat

Trick or Treat

Caroline Crane

DODD, MEAD & COMPANY
New York

Published by Dodd, Mead & Company, Inc.
79 Madison Avenue, New York, N.Y. 10016
Distributed in Canada by
McClelland and Stewart Limited, Toronto
Manufactured in the United States of America
First Edition

Library of Congress Cataloging in Publication Data

Crane, Caroline.
   Trick or treat.

   I. Title.
PS3553.R2695T7   1983   813'.54   83-8998
ISBN 0-396-08217-3

*For
James*

1

He had thought he would never be rid of her. Now, at last, she was leaving the kitchen. His chance had come.

He had everything ready. His poison was a white powder. He could mix it with the sugar. No one would notice.

But not in the sugar bowl. It would have to be a new box. That was part of his plan. He took the bowl from its place on the table and emptied it into the garbage. Then he put it back exactly where it had been.

In the cupboard she had a new one-pound box of Red House sugar. That was one of the things he had been waiting for. He ripped open the pull tab, poured some of the contents into the garbage, and replaced it with his white powder. He stirred it with a table knife, just enough to disguise the powder. Then he put the box on the counter, in plain sight. He didn't think she would remember where it had been before.

He was taking a chance, but not a big one. He knew who was likely to use the sugar next. As for the children, they would have their trick-or-treat candies. They wouldn't be eating sugar out of a box.

He had it all figured out. He had even thought to slip on a pair of plastic gloves before he touched anything.

It was too bad that his ingenuity would have to remain forever anonymous.

Winding Creek Trailer Park lay in a valley betwen the Catskill and the Shawangunk mountains in southern New York State. Theresa and Brian Lonergan had moved there three years ago when their daughter Patty was starting kindergarten. A mobile home had been all they could afford, and Winding Creek was a very attractive park. It looked like a toy village of pastel houses, flowers, shrubs, and shady green lawns. Children could bike and roller-skate on its paved roads, and everybody knew everybody else. It was a good place to live and a good place to raise a family.

Even now, with the leaves and flowers gone for the winter, the place had a tranquil charm. Across the valley, the mountains glowed dull russet with autumn leaves past their prime but not yet fallen. Theresa Lonergan, home from work at three o'clock, drove slowly down the park's front road and stopped beside the mailboxes.

The big yellow school bus had just arrived. Children piled out of it, squealing, shouting, talking excitedly about their plans for Halloween. When Patty appeared, Theresa rolled down the window.

"Mommy, you didn't have to meet me!"

Patty was small for her age, and wore jeans and a pink nylon jacket. Her gray eyes, fringed with long, dark lashes, looked reproachful. Sometimes Patty felt smothered.

2

"I'm not really meeting you. I just stopped to get the mail."
Theresa was aware of her tendency to smother. She could
never get enough of Patty, the only child she would ever
have.

"Well, I'm walking home," Patty announced, and started
down the center road with her friend Bonnie Ann Freaney.

"Okay, I'll see you at the house." Theresa took their mail
from the box and sorted through it. A fuel bill, first delivery of
the season. It wasn't much, because they had filled the tank
last April when the rates were lower. A bank statement. A
shopping circular.

She drove on, overtaking Patty, who pretended not to see
her. She had reached their driveway and parked the car by
the time Patty caught up with her.

"Mommy, we have to finish my dress!"

"I know. Just let me walk the dog and then we'll get right to
it. All we have to do is the hem."

Bonnie Ann asked, "What are you going to be?"

"You'll see," said Patty.

A few weeks earlier, Theresa had taken her to the wedding
of a former baby-sitter. After that, Patty could talk of nothing
but brides and weddings. For Halloween, Theresa had made
her a dress of some inexpensive white lining material. She
bleached a dingy lace curtain to use as a veil, and crowned it
with a wreath of plastic flowers.

"Come on, Mommy, let's go."

"Pat, give me a break." Theresa unlocked the door. Alice,
their part-golden retriever, leaped to meet them, covering
Patty's face with soggy kisses. Patty held her while Theresa
snapped on the leash.

"Hurry back, Mommy."

"I will. Do you have any homework?"

"Only my science questions."

"Okay, you start on those and I'll pin the hem as soon as I
get back." Theresa set off, half walking, half running behind
an eager Alice. When she returned, Patty was wearing the
costume.

3

"You didn't start your homework, did you?" Theresa asked.
"I can do it later."

They shouldn't even give homework on Halloween, Theresa thought as she pinned the dancing, fidgeting dress. Before Patty, she had never realized what a big occasion this was for children.

"Did you used to go trick-or-treating when you were a kid?" Patty asked.

"No." Theresa could not remember much of her childhood, and she couldn't remember trick-or-treating. Knowing Mrs. Sentry, her first foster mother, she thought it unlikely that she had done such a thing. Fortunately, she couldn't even remember Mrs. Sentry very well. She had vague recollections of a strict, distant woman. Of swift rages in which the large, gray-haired creature upon whom she depended seemed terrifyingly out of control. Of a dark place in which she couldn't see anything, but could only feel. She was not even sure the place was real. It might have been a nightmare.

"Why not?" Patty asked.

"Because I lived with a person who didn't believe in it."

"Mrs. Sentry?"

"That's right."

"Why didn't she believe in it?"

Theresa was tired and felt the beginning of a headache. She hated those headaches, implacable and pounding. Brian said they were caused by tension. To her, they felt like migraines.

"Why didn't she?" Patty asked again.

"Because she wasn't that sort of person. She probably thought it was heathen and frivolous."

"What's that mean?"

"Okay, Patty, homework time."

"What does that mean, what you just said?"

There was a time when Theresa would not have believed that a child could drive her crazy. Her own child. Now she believed it, but she would be patient. It wasn't Patty's fault that she was eight years old.

4

"It just means," Theresa said, "that she thought it was silly and maybe a little bit wicked."

"Why did she think it was wicked?"

"Pat, go and get your work done. I have to concentrate on the dress now."

"Can I do it in the living room?"

"In your own room, please, where you can work better."

"I can work okay out here."

"In your own room. That's why Daddy built the desk for you."

Like most children, Patty tried to get away with whatever she could. Theresa had a hard time standing up to her. She felt oddly pleased when she did, almost as though she were being watched and judged.

She wondered if she would ever manage to free herself from that unseen watcher. She didn't even know who it was.

Patty was wearing her costume by the time Brian came home from work. He stood in the doorway while she waltzed about the living room, showing it off. He was wearing his tan suede jacket and Theresa thought he looked exceptionally handsome. It set off his hair, which was nearly the same shade as the jacket, but more golden, and brought a vibrant glow to his face. She remembered how upset she had been when she learned the number of women customers he had. She had always thought of Reynolds as a lumberyard. But it was combined with a home improvement center, and he worked inside, where most of the women shopped.

"Look, Daddy, my beautiful dress. Mommy made it."

"Very nice," said Brian. "Very pretty on you." Then he ruined it all by asking, "What are you supposed to be? A ghost?"

"A bride. What's the matter with you, Daddy?"

"Bride of Dracula?"

"Just a bride."

"How come you haven't left yet?" he asked. "It's late and it's getting dark."

"It's more fun in the dark."

"Uh—" He looked past her at Theresa.

"Well, you see," Theresa explained, "in the afternoon there aren't enough people around, so they wouldn't get much of anything. But we'll have an early dinner and then they're going out at six."

Brian still seemed uneasy. "Shall I go with her?"

Patty groaned. Theresa said, "No, really, she'll be all right. She's going with Bonnie Ann and some of the others, and they'll end up at the Freaneys' for a little while. Don't you think that's okay?"

The Freaneys lived in Number 46, right across the road. He guessed it was okay. He went to wash up while Patty set the table and Theresa put together a salad to go with her noodle casserole. Patty ate quickly and did not wait for dessert.

"Canned pears," she said, wrinkling her nose.

"If it was lime pie, I'll bet you'd stay," replied Theresa.

"Can we have lime pie tomorrow? I gotta go now, it's almost six." Patty ran to the bedroom for her coat.

"Keep that buttoned while you're outside," Theresa told her. "It's pretty chilly. And have fun."

Brian said, "You won't go out of the park, will you, babe? And you'll come home early."

"Yes, remember it's a school night," Theresa added. Patty endured their precautions and admonitions and finally escaped, carrying a paper shopping bag that she hoped to fill with candy and gum. Theresa stood on the steps, watching her dash across the road and up to the Freaneys' sun deck. The door opened and Patty vanished.

Theresa let the storm door close behind her and stood outside in her thin sweater, feeling the clear cold of the early night air. She breathed deeply to savor the fragrance of smoke from wood-burning stoves. Another winter was on its way.

She looked forward to it, as she did to summer. Winters in the mountains were often cold and snowy, but their trailer was cosy and she loved every part of the year. She loved Brian and Patty and their life together. Everything, except the spells of forgetfulness and the nightmares that came to her sometimes, even with Brian there beside her. The dreams of dark places and an invisible presence.

"Hey," he said, opening the door. "You trying to get sick or something?"

"Don't take me away from that gorgeous smell," she protested as she followed him inside.

"I'm going to take you all the way back there." He propelled her toward their bedroom at the rear of the trailer.

"We can't right now, Brian."

"Not another headache?"

"No, because of the kids. There'll be ten thousand kids coming to the door. Do you want them to go home and tell their parents?"

"Their parents don't know we fool around sometimes?"

"Brian!" She ducked under his arm and went to answer the door. She had heard their voices, even if he hadn't.

"Trick or treat!"

Patty, in her white dress and pink jacket, stood on the steps with two witches, a robot, and a hobo. Theresa brought them a mixing bowl filled with miniature chocolate bars. "One for each of you," she told them. "There have to be enough for the other kids."

The children took turns reaching into the bowl. First Bonnie Ann, then Patty, then Lisa Stevens, and awkward Mark Freaney, the hobo, who was twelve years old and should have been out with children his own age. Last of all came the robot. He grabbed two bars and scuttled down the steps before she could stop him.

In a laughing, chattering group, they went on to the next house. Theresa watched them until Patty's dress, glowing like a pale beacon, faded into the autumn dusk.

3

Patty's shopping bag was half filled by the time they had visited every home in the park. She was glad they were going to the Freaneys' for a while. She was not yet ready to end this enchanted evening. This beautiful, magical night, with jack-o'-lanterns flickering in windows and entryways, and groups of costumed children roaming the roads and paths. For a few hours, the world belonged to them.

They walked in a line that stretched across the road, she and Gus and Lisa and Bonnie Ann. Mark Freaney had gone off with another boy and it was more fun without him. He was too old for them, always trying to show off that he was better and knew more things. She suspected that he was a little bit embarrassed when he had to hang out with Bonnie and her friends.

"Now I'll get to take off my coat so you can see my whole costume," she told Bonnie, who was dressed as a witch, with a frizzy gray wig and a face smeared with lip liner.

Enviously Bonnie eyed the white dress. "Where did you get that costume?"

"My mother made it," Patty replied, uncertain as to whether that was a plus or a minus.

"My mother could do that," Bonnie said, assuring herself. The four of them clattered up the wooden steps to the sun deck and into the Freaneys' kitchen-dining room.

8

Mark and his friend, a boy named John, were there ahead of them. John wore a long, black cape and was playing with a knife.

"Hey, look at this!" Mark grabbed the knife and plunged it into his chest. Lisa screamed.

Mark laughed as he held it up. "Look, it telescopes inside itself. Makes it look real."

Mrs. Freaney shouted above the noise, "That's enough of that. It's disgusting. John, put away the knife."

Mr. Freaney didn't seem to be there at all, and Patty was glad. Nothing was ever nice when he was around. He yelled at Bonnie and Mark and sometimes hit them. He said mean things that embarrassed them in front of their friends and then demanded to know why they couldn't take a joke.

The children milled about the table, where there was a plate of bakery cookies. Some of the children had cans of soda. Anybody who could get close to Mrs. Freaney and the refrigerator could have a can of soda, but the kitchen was small and crowded with seven people, and Patty had to wait.

She looked inside her bag. "Oh, goodie, lime!" She pounced on a package of three flower-shaped jellies in different colors. "I love lime," she announced to no one in particular as she opened the package and took out the green daisy.

"Better than chocolate?" Lisa asked.

Patty took a bite of her lime candy. Her mouth puckered and she swallowed quickly. It was not at all what she had expected. The lime was pungent and deep-flavored, but the candy itself was sour. She saw no reason at all for sour candy.

She was about to discard it when she noticed the perfect solution. A box of sugar on the counter. That was all it needed.

"I'll just put some of this on," she muttered as she lifted the lid of the box, dipped in her daisy and scooped up a mound of sugar.

One of the children let out a yelp. She turned to see what was happening, holding the candy cupped in her hands so the sugar would not fall off.

9

It was Gus Bova. He had removed his robot headpiece and was probing his mouth with a messy finger. She saw blood on his teeth mixed with the chocolate.

Mrs. Freaney bent down to see his mouth, then snatched a half-eaten candy bar out of his hand. "Oh, my God!"

Patty edged closer and stared, while she absentmindedly stuffed the rest of the daisy into her mouth.

Suddenly her attention was all on herself. She had expected to savor the lime, but instead found her mouth full of bitterness. A horrid, sickening bitterness, much worse than before. She couldn't reach the garbage to spit it out. Mrs. Freaney and Gus were in the way. Gagging, she managed to swallow it.

"Eeeeuu," she said as she gasped for breath. "That's yucky." She needed something to wash the taste away. She tugged at Mrs. Freaney's sleeve and asked timidly, "Can I please have a Coke or something?"

"Not now, for heaven's sake." Cheryl Freaney was busy dismembering Gus's chocolate bar. "A needle! Oh, God, how can people do these things? Gussie, where did you get this?"

Gus looked at her in bewilderment. "I dunno."

Patty backed away from them. She felt terrible. As if she were going to be sick. She couldn't understand it. Just because of a sour candy. She clamped her hand over her mouth and retched. She retched again as she stumbled down the hall toward the bathroom.

Cheryl caught herself screaming at Gus. "Don't you remember who gave it to you? Are you stupid or what?"

She tried to regain her self-control. It wasn't his fault. Why frighten him further? This was what came of living with a man like Leonard.

"I dunno where I got it."

She had to be rational. Of course he didn't know. They must have canvased fifty to a hundred houses, and these things didn't come with labels on them. What should she do?

Call the police? Was it serious enough for that, or would they laugh at her?

Bonnie Ann grabbed her arm. "Mommy, come and look at Patty!"

Cheryl raised a hand to brush away or slap the child. She stopped when she saw that this was no game. Bonnie's eyes were round and fearful.

"What's wrong with Patty?"

"She's in the bathroom. She's sick."

From too much candy, Cheryl thought, but Bonnie's urgency forced her down the hallway. Patty was lying on the bathroom floor.

"Oh, my God!"

She knelt beside the girl. Patty's eyes were closed. Bubbles of saliva appeared between her lips.

"Patty? Patty?" She touched her cheek. Patty's head rolled to one side.

Cheryl looked up. The children were clustered in the doorway, watching.

"What happened?" she demanded.

"I don't know," said Bonnie.

"Doesn't anybody know anything?" She rose to her feet. The police. No, the first aid squad. She had their number pasted beside the telephone, just in case. "Stay with her," she told Bonnie as she hurried to the living room. She dialed the number with fumbling hands.

"Hello? Hello? This is Winding Creek Trailer Park, Number Forty-six, third row. There's a child here—she fainted. She's foaming at the mouth. Come quick!"

A child. Fainted. It was worse than that. Deep down, she knew it. Maybe the suddenness. The foaming.

She went back to Patty. The girl had stopped breathing. Oh, my God.

It couldn't be happening. It shouldn't. It was as if someone had put in the wrong film. She could back up the projector. Start again.

11

She brushed away the saliva and put her mouth to Patty's. She didn't know quite how to do this. She forced her own breath into Patty's mouth. She wasn't sure it would work. But then Patty took a breath on her own.

Cheryl sat up. "Bonnie Ann—somebody—Mark—go over and get Patty's mom."

She didn't want Theresa to know. But they had to know. And Theresa was a nurse. A licensed practical nurse. She should have thought of it before.

"Mark, wait outside to catch the ambulance," she said. It was dark. The ambulance would have to slow down, watching for numbers. They couldn't afford that.

It should take them about five minutes to drive from the village. Once they came, it would be their responsibility. She couldn't handle it alone. And Patty had stopped breathing again.

She heard a door slam and running footsteps. Then Brian and Theresa were there. She stood back. Brian lifted Patty out into the hall where there was more room. He called and coaxed his daughter. Cheryl said, "A stroke of some kind."

She had no idea why she said it. She didn't even know whether a child could have a stroke, but it didn't matter what she said. No one paid attention.

Theresa was working over the girl, trying to make her breathe.

"There's a heartbeat," Brian said, feeling the small wrist. "If we can keep her breathing. What happened?"

"I don't know," answered Cheryl. "She just collapsed. They should be here any minute." It seemed to take forever. It couldn't have been only a few minutes ago that she had called them.

"What do you mean?" asked Brian. "She just fainted?"

"She didn't feel good," said one of the children. "She came in here and then she fell. I saw her grab onto the sink."

"Grab onto the sink?"

"To keep from falling."

Cheryl raised her head. Far in the distance she heard the

12

whoop of a siren. Thank God. Now, whatever happened, it would be out of her hands.

They came in with a stretcher. She herded the children into the living room. They wanted to watch. She turned on the television. They flocked to the bay window that overlooked the road. The gleaming ambulance with its flashing red light seemed huge and alien, like a misplaced space vehicle.

The men were in the kitchen, strapping Patty to a stretcher. She heard something about "oxygen." It meant Patty was still alive, and now that help was here, everything would be all right. But it took so long. She wished they would hurry and get out. She peered around the living room door. They were almost ready to leave. She saw them out and then went back to the window.

She couldn't tell much about Patty. They had covered her with a blanket and put an oxygen mask over her face. Cheryl saw Brian run into his own house. A moment later he was back, getting into his car and starting the engine. Theresa followed the stretcher into the ambulance. Then there was more delay. Patiently Brian ran his engine. A person could die ten times before they ever got going.

And then the ambulance started off, silently at first, picking up speed. Brian turned out of his driveway and followed it. The space vehicle shot down the road and turned a corner, with Brian racing after it. She heard the siren start up as the flashing red lights disappeared among the trees.

Theresa looked down at the pale face, which she could barely see under the oxygen mask. Her daughter. Her only child. She couldn't believe it. What had happened? Had she made the costume too tight? She reached over to feel the neckline, knowing all along that that was not the trouble and she didn't want to face what had happened.

The ambulance attendant said, "It's okay, ma'am. We'll be there in a coupla minutes."

She didn't believe that, either. Valley Center was a good

twelve miles away. Everybody was saying things, meaningless things. And she didn't understand what had happened. "Coupla minutes," he repeated.

She looked out at the familiar road. They were rounding the bend where the egg farm was. And then the dark woods again. Racing through the night. A dream. Dark places. She dreamed of dark places sometimes, but in those dreams, she was standing still.

She held Patty's hand, feeling suspended in time. She had to, because time was what counted. She couldn't let any more of it go by.

She thought of Brian, following behind. She couldn't have done it herself, driven the car. She'd have fallen apart, but Brian could do it. She couldn't see him from where she sat, but she knew he was there.

The attendant picked up Patty's other hand and felt for her pulse. Then, with his thumb, he gently raised one of her eyelids. He glanced at Theresa and quickly looked away.

She felt something cold begin to spread through her. Instantly she rejected it. Everything would come out all right.

Or maybe it wouldn't. She had been so happy these last ten years. Now she had to pay for it. She should have known it couldn't last. Maybe she had known. Every so often she would catch herself, and be afraid.

She wouldn't think about it now. She stopped thinking altogether and simply held Patty's hand, not daring to feel for a pulse beat. And after a while she saw the lights of Valley Center.

She willed the ambulance down each street and around each corner. She willed it into the emergency bay at the hospital. Then she was hurrying down a corridor, trying to keep up with a gurney that bore her daughter. But the gurney went through a pair of double doors and the doors closed in her face.

A nurse took her arm. "Why don't you wait out here, dear? Can I get you anything?"

"I want to be with her," Theresa said. Every part of her body seemed detached and meaningless.

"It'll only be a minute." Why did everybody tell these lies? The nurse showed her to a small waiting room, just an alcove off the corridor. No one else was there. Theresa sat down on an upholstered bench.

"I don't understand what happened," she told the nurse. She had an idea, but she couldn't think about it. It didn't make sense.

"Did she ever have anything like this before?"

"No, nothing."

Not fits. Not fainting. Not epilepsy. It was none of those, so why should Patty have had it before?

The nurse excused herself and left. Nurses were always busy. The very fact that she had stayed for even a moment seemed ominous. Theresa waited, not thinking. Not allowing anything to go through her mind.

Someone was coming down the hall. She knew his walk. She was not aware of standing up, but suddenly she was in his arms.

"I had to do all the admissions stuff," he explained. "The insurance."

"Admissions?" That meant Patty was going to stay for a while. She would get well!

"You'd think in an emergency they could wait a little," he added.

They held each other, and listened and watched, but no one came to tell them what was happening. After a while, when they had each seemed to gain some strength from the other, they sat down together on the bench.

She wanted to talk. If they talked about Patty, it would make her real again.

"She was so proud of that costume," Theresa said.

He nodded, staring at the floor. She remembered that Patty's veil had fallen off, and the wreath. Left behind in the Freaneys' bathroom.

15

She had been perfectly well only two hours before, when they started out trick-or-treating. When Theresa watched them go off into the dusk. In those two hours, what had happened? They said it was sudden. Maybe a sudden, devastating virus? Was there anything like that outside of science fiction? Why hadn't anybody else gotten it?

Something in the candy. That was what she didn't want to think about. It would be her fault, for allowing Patty to go out, but how could she have known?

She should have known. She knew about the crazies who put razor blades in apples.

Maybe an allergy. The sugar, perhaps. Patty was a sugar freak.

She got up from the bench. She must tell them. Patty was a sugar freak. She loved candy and sugar, and maybe it all got to be too much for her. Maybe it was like a diabetic coma.

Across the hall, the double doors opened and a white-coated man came out. He had wiry blond hair and a somber expression.

"Mr. and Mrs. Lonergan? I'm Dr. Eastman." He walked over to where they stood, put one hand on Brian's shoulder, the other on hers.

"We did everything we could," he said, "but I'm afraid it was too late."

A buzzing started in her head. She felt herself, sinking, fading.

"How could it be too late?" she asked.

And she remembered that she had known, even in the ambulance.

"I'm sorry." His hand pressed her shoulder.

Brian asked angrily, "What do you mean there was nothing you could do?"

"I know what you're feeling," said the doctor. "I'd give anything if I could have come out here with a different report."

She thought how artificial his words sounded, but they

16

were probably true. Yet she didn't understand how they could have let Patty die.

"I don't understand," she said.

"We're all kind of stunned," replied the doctor. She wasn't sure what he meant. "It seems to have been a cardiopulmonary collapse. Very, very sudden. There was nothing anybody could have done."

Cardiopulmonary meant the heart and lungs. It couldn't have been that. Her system wouldn't have collapsed for no reason.

She wondered why she felt so numb. So insulated.

"Do you mean," she asked, "that my daughter just—died?" She forced herself to say it and felt she was being courageous, but the word was only an empty sound.

Brian said, "She wasn't even sick."

"No. She wouldn't have to be," the doctor agreed. "I noticed she was wearing some kind of costume. Was she trick-or-treating?"

Theresa nodded, afraid of what he was getting at. He went on, "Did she eat any of the candy?"

"I don't know. She was at someone else's house. They called us over."

Brian folded his arms tightly. "You're not saying it was the candy."

"We don't have the lab report, of course," the doctor replied, "but the symptoms are indicative of poisoning. A very powerful, fast-acting poison."

"But it couldn't be!" cried Theresa. "Not in our park! We live in a trailer park, in Pine Glen. We know the people there. They wouldn't—"

"There will certainly be an investigation," said the doctor. "Tell me, did she vomit or anything?"

Theresa turned away. She didn't want to hear any more. Brian said, "My wife already told you we weren't there. It was somebody else's house. By the time they called us over, she was on the floor. She wasn't even breathing. Maybe if—"

17

He stopped. Theresa said, "If they'd called us sooner."

The doctor shook his head. "If it's what I think it is, and I think it might be cyanide or something like that, there wouldn't have been anything anybody could do. She never had a chance."

Never had a chance . . . It wasn't possible that it was really all over. Of course she had a chance.

Brian asked, "Is she—still here? Could we see her?"

"Certainly." The doctor pushed open one of the double doors and stood back to let them go ahead of him. They walked down a corridor to a glass-walled anteroom, through another door to a brightly lit, windowless cubicle. In the center of the cubicle was a metal table with a sheeted figure on it.

The doctor left them alone in the small room. They stood together, staring at the sheet. Once they lifted it and saw her dead, then she would really be dead.

Finally Brian approached the table. With Theresa beside him, he drew back the sheet. They both stood looking down at her, at the pale face, the closed eyes. More than asleep. At the tumbled brown hair, a shade lighter than Theresa's and darker than Brian's.

Theresa reached out and touched the cheek. She had thought it would be cold, but it was warm. She bent down and kissed her child's forehead. Then she stepped back to make room for Brian.

"I still can't believe it," she said. "I just don't believe this."

Brian replied huskily, "I know. I keep thinking there must be some way we can take her home and have everything— everything—"

They stood together, holding each other's hand and looking down at their daughter. They didn't want the time to end, but it had already ended. Finally they turned away and left the room.

The doctor, who had waited at a discreet distance, accompanied them outside. When they reached the corridor, they found Cheryl Freaney pacing back and forth. She rushed toward them, holding out her arms. "Oh, how is she?"

They stood and looked at her. It was such an irrelevant question.

"Oh, no," Cheryl gasped, retreating. "Oh, don't tell me. No." She turned to the doctor. He nodded his head very slightly, as though he didn't want the Lonergans to overhear.

Cheryl's eyes were huge and blue, and she wore her blond hair in a slightly off-center knot at the back of her head. From the depths of her soul, Theresa felt hatred rising.

Cheryl must have seen it. Her face slackened with alarm. Again she turned to the doctor. "But how did it happen? She was right there in my house. She was perfectly all right."

The doctor took her elbow and led her away, speaking in low tones. They saw Cheryl shake her head. He was probably asking about the vomiting. Theresa looked at her husband, but knew he couldn't help her. At that moment, she didn't feel anything for him. She couldn't even feel herself. It was as though her life had suddenly ended in a gray void.

She fought waking up. Tried to will herself back into the dark room. She knew there was some terrible reason why she did not want to be conscious.

The doctor had given them sleeping pills. Two each, and they had taken them all. She hadn't thought it would do any good.

But it did, and she had had the dream again. The dream of a dark room, a black, black room, and someone else was there. Someone in the room with her. She could only sense it. Someone she didn't know. She had heard a voice trying to tell her something, but now the words were gone.

Suddenly she remembered what she had tried to forget. "Patty!" she cried aloud.

Beside her, the bed moved. Brian woke and looked at her. Then he, too, remembered. He closed his eyes and sank back with a wrenching moan.

It couldn't be true, Theresa thought. It was too horrible to be true.

Like the dark room. The real dark room, where Mrs. Sentry used to lock her as a punishment. It was almost all she could remember of her childhood.

"I can't sleep any more," she said, sitting up. She wished there had been more pills. It was already daylight, but all she wanted to do from now on was sleep.

He mumbled something. She sat on the edge of the bed. Across the room she could see a pale stain on the brown carpet. When Patty was five years old, she had spilled white shoe polish there. Theresa had never been able to get it all out. And ever afterward, even knowing it was there, she would mistake that stain for a patch of sunlight.

She got up and walked down the hallway to the living room, stepping around Alice, who lay beside the closed door to Patty's room. She looked at the familiar furniture. There was something about it that did not feel like her house.

Because Patty was gone. Forever.

And then she found it. A very faint smell of cigarette smoke in the air. Their house did not smell of cigarettes, except when they had guests. In the ashtray on the table by the sofa there were four filter-tipped butts. She flushed them down the toilet. She was always afraid of fire if she put them in the garbage.

Brian came out of the bedroom. "What was that, hon?"

"Nothing." She concealed the ashtray in the folds of her bathrobe and took it back to the living room.

He followed her. "I thought maybe you were sick or something."

"How do you expect me to feel?"

She shouldn't have said it that way. She didn't mean to rebuff him.

"Do you want me to make coffee?" she asked.

"If you feel up to it."

She wondered why they would want to drink coffee. She never wanted to eat or drink again.

Does it ever get better? she wondered. Ever?

She set up the coffee maker and plugged it in. Now what? Maybe he would want breakfast. He always liked to cook his own eggs.

He had gone back to put on his robe. She heard water running in the bathroom. A few minutes later he joined her. "What's that smell?" he asked.

21

"Coffee."

"I thought I smelled cigarettes."

She said nothing. If she didn't answer, he would drop the subject. She stared out of the window. In the distance, someone in a red jacket was walking up the road.

She looked at the clock on the stove. Seven-thirty. She hadn't known it was so late. The children would all be trooping up to the school bus. She closed the curtains and turned on the cold water as far as it would go.

"What did you do that for?" Brian asked.

"I don't want to hear them."

After a moment he realized what she meant. "It's going to be hard," he said.

She turned off the water and poured the coffee. She couldn't touch hers. Brian fried an egg for himself, mixed the orange juice, and made some toast. She was grateful that he didn't urge her to eat.

"Did you call Nancy?" he asked.

She looked up, shocked. She had forgotten about Nancy Schwartz, the woman she worked for, a young mother with multiple sclerosis.

She pictured herself saying the words. "I won't be able to come today. My daughter died last night."

"I can't do it."

"Okay." He got up from the table. "What's her number?"

She gave him the number and put her hands over her ears while he made the call. She kept them there until he finished.

He noticed. "You didn't want to hear me say it."

No, she hadn't. "Brian, what are we going to do?"

"We'll have to take it one day at a time," he said.

It wasn't really an answer, and that was the hell of it. There was nothing they could do.

"Do you realize," he said, "that our daughter was probably murdered? If it was a powerful poison like the doctor said, that was no accident. And there's nothing we can do."

22

It was exactly what she had been thinking. Nothing they could do.

He looked down at his hands resting on the table. They were strong hands, square hands with squared-off fingertips. He flexed his fingers, then curled them into a fist.

People weren't supposed to do nothing. People were supposed to fight back.

"Did you hear me?" he said. "If it was a powerful, fast-acting poison—"

"He said there would be an investigation."

"Sure they'll investigate. Do you think they can find anybody like that? I just wish I knew who it was."

Theresa sat staring at her coffee. She was closing more and more into herself. She could feel it.

"I wish I knew who it was," he said again. "It'd be interesting to know what sort of person would do a thing like that."

"Brian, there are so many crazy people."

"This is more than just a crazy person. Most crazy people never do any harm. Eight lousy years," he went on. "She should have had a lifetime."

Theresa's voice trembled. "They were good years."

"Okay, you know what I mean. She was cheated out of her life. And look what they've done to us."

"I can't feel angry yet," she said.

"I can. And you will. It's a funny thing, Theresa. The person who did it, I almost feel as if there's some kind of thread, something that goes from him to us. Because he killed our daughter. Hell, it must have been somebody here in this park."

"I just don't see how. These people are all—they're all decent."

"Okay, I suppose it could have happened outside. Maybe the candy was poisoned before it got here. In the store, or someplace. But look, he knows who he is. He's got a consciousness and so have I. He knows about us, even if we don't

23

know him. He'll be thinking about us. There's got to be some kind of invisible—thing. A mind thing, you know what I mean? There must be some way to tune into that, to connect up with him and find him."

"Maybe."

"I've got to know who it is," he said.

5

Cheryl Freaney skirted around the breakfast table, trying not to disturb her husband. Leonard was in one of his silent moods. His face was pale, his lips tight. As usual, there was a self-important pride in his anger. He had to let them all know how he felt.

It was probably because of what happened last night, but she didn't see how he could blame her. Or even Patty. The unfortunate fact was that Leonard's moods had nothing to do with reason.

And she needed someone to talk to.

He was paging through the *Journal*, which was delivered to their door each morning. She saw his head jerk forward. Then he slammed the paper with his hand.

"How the hell did this guy get hold of it so fast? He's got a hot line, or something?"

She looked over his shoulder. Maynard Bundy. She never liked Bundy's columns and rarely bothered to read them. He tended to sensationalize everything, even tragedy.

There it was. All that had happened to her last night. The needle in Gus's chocolate bar. Patty's death. Somehow Bundy knew it was cyanide, even though Cheryl herself wasn't sure because the doctor hadn't been certain when she talked to him.

There was everything but her name. She felt a flash of disappointment, and then decided it was probably just as well. She would not have wanted her name broadcast with all those terrible things. Certainly Leonard wouldn't want it.

"He must have stayed up all night writing the column," she commented mildly.

Leonard slapped the paper again, this time with the back of his hand. "How'd they get hold of it?" His eyes narrowed. "Did you call the paper?"

"Why would I do that?" she demanded angrily.

"To get yourself famous."

She was hurt. But not really surprised. Leonard had a knack for thinking the worst of people, even of her. Perhaps especially of her. People asked her sometimes why she put up with him. It was none of their business.

"What does he say?" she asked.

"The usual crap. All the crap about what kind of world we're handing to our children. Friends and neighbors become The Enemy. Childhood pastime turns into homicide. It's a lotta bull." He glared and asked again, "How'd they find out?"

"Maybe from the police," she said. "I know reporters often hang around the police, because that's where the news is."

"Police? Are you crazy or just stupid?"

"What do you mean?" She was fed up with his constant blame. "I didn't have anything to do with that! When I went to the hospital last night, the doctor told me he thought it was poison. Of course he had to call the police. And of course they had to talk to me. I was the only one here when it happened."

"Oh, boy." He closed the newspaper and pushed back his chair. "I still don't see why you had to get involved."

"Oh, sure, I planned the whole thing."

"Well, you didn't have to have all those kids over here."

"How the hell did I know what was going to happen? And Bonnie and Mark deserve some fun."

"Some fun," he mimicked. "What do they ever do to earn it?"

"Don't be so damn grouchy. You could have fun, too, if you

26

weren't always in a temper." She swept past him, swaying in her satin housecoat to show him what kind of fun she had in mind. And then she thought of Patty, and was ashamed.

And Theresa and Brian. She could scarcely keep from looking out at their trailer to see what they were doing this morning. She hadn't expected them to go to work, but there seemed to be no sign of life at all. The kitchen curtains were still drawn. She wondered if they could possibly have killed themselves. She wondered what a person would do if their only child died.

Leonard left for work and she was alone. Bonnie hadn't wanted to go to school that morning, but Cheryl felt it would be morbid if she stayed home. It was better to keep on with her normal routine.

She poured herself another cup of coffee and sat down at the table. It was her peaceful time, before she started the laundry. But it couldn't be peaceful today, because of—

Because there was a car stopping outside. She jumped up, hoping it was only Leonard coming back for something.

It was a police car, parking in front of the Lonergans' driveway. A man got out and walked up the path to their door.

She dashed to her living room for a better look. She saw the Lonergans' door open, but not who opened it. The man went inside.

A police investigator. He would probably come and talk to her again and Leonard would be angry, if he found out.

"Don't get involved," Leonard would say. As if anyone had given her a choice!

She hurried back to the bedroom, sloughed off her housecoat and put on a sweatshirt and a pair of jeans. No sense appearing in her slinky satin and giving him the wrong idea.

She had washed the breakfast dishes and was sorting the laundry by the time he arrived at her door.

"Police," he said, in case she hadn't guessed. His name was Jess Morehouse. It struck her as appropriate, because he was as big as a house.

"I guess it's about what happened last night," she babbled,

wondering why policemen all looked basically alike. They all had mustaches and the same kind of haircut.

"Right," said Morehouse. "I'd like to ask you a few questions, okay?"

"Sure. Come in." She stood back to admit him. She didn't care for that line, "I'd like to ask you a few questions." On television, it was what they said to the suspects.

She led him into her living room. "Would you like some coffee?" she asked nervously, not knowing what was expected of her.

He sat down, declining the coffee, and opened a notepad. He began by asking her name, her husband's name, and where they both worked. He liked to get a general picture, he said.

"Uh—" Her mouth felt dry. "I don't work anywhere. I mean I work here. I'm a housewife." She couldn't understand why he needed to know those things, why he wanted a general picture of her and Leonard, unless he thought they had something to do with it.

"And your husband?"

"He works in Valley Center. At Scalzo Motors. He's a salesman."

"How long has he been there?"

"Oh. Gee. Five years?"

"And how long have you lived at this address?"

"Five years, I guess. They were both about the same time."

"Any children?"

"Yes, two, a boy and a girl. Mark is twelve and Bonnie Ann's eight."

"They go to school?"

"Yes. In Valley Center." She tried to speak naturally, to show him she had nothing to hide. But all the questions made her so nervous that she felt as though she were floating away.

He uncrossed and recrossed his long legs. "You had two incidents here last night," he said.

"Two?" She had forgotten about Gus. "Oh. The needle. Oh,

lord." And she remembered how Patty had tugged at her arm and asked for a drink of Coke and Cheryl had brushed her aside. That was what she had wanted to talk about to Leonard. She felt so terrible. And it must have been after Patty had taken the poison, because Cheryl had asked the doctor what it tasted like, and he said if it was cyanide, it was bitter. And she had been busy with Gus, and then the child had died, and, oh God, she didn't even want to think about it.

He asked her where the chocolate bar had come from. How could he care about that, when Patty was dead?

"I don't know," she said. "He had it all in a bag. I don't know who gave it to him, and he didn't, either. I asked."

"Was it candy he'd collected when he was trick-or-treating? Did you give the children any candy?"

"Yes, when they came to the door, but it wasn't that. Not Moon Bars. I had a bag of Milky Ways and that peanut butter thing. They were miniatures, in bags. Two bags. The Moon Bar was full-size. I can't imagine anybody giving out full-size bars at Halloween, they're too expensive." She tried to laugh.

"How did you know it was a Moon Bar?"

"He had a wrapper. You could see a little hole in it where somebody pushed the needle through."

She felt faint. The whole thing made her ill. But it was not nearly as bad as what happened to Patty.

"Did you save the wrapper?"

"I don't know. I guess it's somewhere. I mean, after Patty—the little girl who died—"

"Yes, I'm coming to that."

"I don't see how anybody could do a thing like that. How could they?"

"Did the children at any time go outside this trailer park?"

"You mean trick-or-treating? I don't think so. There's enough people right here, and you can see, out on the highway, there's only one house in walking distance. But I don't see how it could be anybody here. They're all so nice, and a person would have to be crazy—"

29

A person would have to be crazy.

"There just isn't anybody like that here," she concluded.

She had meant that a person would have to be crazy to pull something like that in such a limited area. They would certainly be found out sooner or later.

"Let me get the sequence of events now," said Morehouse. "The children went out trick-or-treating. What time did they start?"

"About six."

"Did they go in a group? How many?"

"Well, they started out together, but my son came back separately with his friend John Reiss. The other kids—there were four. My daughter Bonnie, and Lisa Stevens, and Gus Bova. He's the one who got the needle. And Patty Lonergan."

"How long were they out? The group with your daughter."

"About an hour and a half, maybe two hours. Then they came back here. We were going to have a little party, just for a while. It was a school night, but you know how kids love Halloween. I had cookies and soda, but I figured they were mostly going to sit around and eat their candy."

"Your call to the first aid squad came a little before eight."

"Yes. The kids just got here. They were all in the kitchen. Some of them started eating their candy. Then Gus made a noise and his mouth was all bloody. I'd heard stories, so I took the candy away from him and found the needle. Then my daughter said 'Come look at Patty,' and she was on the bathroom floor. I tried—she wasn't breathing too well. I tried to make her breathe, and I sent the kids to get her parents. And I called the first aid squad."

Morehouse was writing it all in his notepad. "What was the Lonergan girl eating when she collapsed, do you know?"

"I don't know. I didn't see the wrapper. I didn't look. I was just trying to make her breathe."

"Did you throw out any of the trash from last night?"

"No, it's in a can under the sink. I cleaned up the kitchen. I didn't know she was going to die. I just thought—"

30

"That's understandable, Mrs. Freaney. Nobody knew right off it was a possible homicide, or we would have come last night."

And wouldn't Leonard have loved that, coming home from his bowling night to find the kitchen full of policemen. It had been bad enough as it was.

"Maybe if you come back this afternoon," she suggested, "when the children get home from school, maybe you can ask if anybody saw what she was eating."

He nodded and went on writing. Of course he would have thought of it. He was a trained investigator.

He left, taking with him the trash bag from under the sink, as well as Patty's trick-or-treat bag, which Cheryl had tossed in beside it. He praised her for saving everything. She hadn't really meant to save it. Just hadn't gotten around to dumping it out. She was glad she had done something right, even inadvertently. She couldn't help feeling that she was under some kind of cloud. Maybe it was natural, in her position.

She followed him out to the sun deck, rolled her eyes toward the Lonergans' trailer, and asked in a low voice, "How are they taking it?"

"How do you think?" Morehouse replied.

Again she felt ashamed. It was a stupid, gossipy question. He would think her a real bubblebrain. She went back to the kitchen and sat down in one of the dinette chairs. Maybe some hot cocoa would be nice. Or even a glass of wine. How could this thing have happened to her? In her house? It wasn't fair. She had only wanted to give the children a good time.

The telephone rang. Oh, no, the police again? The hospital? Maybe it was all a mistake and Patty hadn't died after all.

It was Marylou Grover from Number 43.

"I heard what happened," Marylou said, "and I just saw the cop leave. I don't dare call Theresa. How are they, do you know?"

"Pretty awful, I guess. I haven't been over there. I keep

31

feeling as if—well, you know, it happened right here under my nose. I keep feeling as if I should have done something."

"You couldn't have known," said Marylou. "Do you need a shoulder? Or an ear?"

"Oh, God. Come over. I'll make some coffee."

This was what she needed. Not the coffee, it would make her climb the wall. She needed a person.

Marylou arrived a few minutes later with her two-year-old son Alex. She had another child in school and was expecting a third in a few months.

"I can't believe it," she said as she sat down at the table. "I can't believe anybody could do a thing like that, putting poison in a child's candy. And lethal poison. Can you imagine? How can people be so sick? It couldn't have been anybody here."

"In the park, you mean?" Cheryl didn't want to talk about it, but probably it was the only thing people were going to talk about for a while.

"I really can't believe it." Marylou shook her head. "That poor little girl, just blown away like that. It's incredible. You can bet my kids are never going trick-or-treating again. Just think, it could have happened to any of them. I can't get over it."

"Neither can I," Cheryl said.

"Those poor people. Their only child. I wonder if they'll have another one now."

"They can't," said Cheryl. "I don't know what the problem is, but I know they can't have more. She had several miscarriages before Patty."

"Oh, no! It really isn't fair. And there are people having babies they don't even want. Alex, you play with the cars we brought and stay out of Cheryl's cupboards." Marylou handed her son a paper bag full of toys.

"I feel so awful," Cheryl said, joining her friend at the table while the coffeemaker steamed and dripped. "I couldn't tell Theresa. Or even the police, because it might get back."

Marylou's eyes widened. Cheryl said quickly, "It's nothing

like that. I didn't do anything. But I have to get this off my chest and then I don't want to talk about the Lonergans ever again."

She told Marylou about Patty's wanting the Coke. "And I was busy with Gus. I couldn't—"

"It probably wouldn't have made any difference."

"No, but it was the last thing she ever wanted in her whole life." Cheryl pressed her hand to her mouth.

"Oh, honey." Marylou got up from her chair and gave her a hug. "I'm glad I came. You do need a shoulder. This whole thing must be awful for you."

Cheryl sniffled for a while and then poured the coffee. "I'm glad you came, too. It does help to talk. I couldn't even tell that to Leonard. He was in one of his moods."

Marylou knew what she meant. Leonard was so often in one of his moods. No one quite understood how Cheryl put up with him, or why, but she supposed there were reasons. He was a strong figure, if irrational at times, and a good, solid provider.

Cheryl was reaching toward the refrigerator to get out the milk when the telephone rang. "Excuse me," she said, and went to the living room to answer it. Marylou got out the milk herself and opened the sugar bowl. It was empty, but there was a box of sugar on the counter. She poured milk into her coffee and added two spoonfuls of sugar.

She thought the coffee smelled a little strange when she picked it up. It must have been the milk. She sniffed the carton. It didn't seem to be spoiled. She drank some of the coffee. It didn't taste right, either. Maybe it was stale. She didn't want to tell Cheryl and embarrass her. Instead she added more sugar and tried it again. It was still awful. But she would be polite about it. Alex, making engine noises, ran a plastic car over her foot.

Cheryl seemed to stay on the phone forever. Marylou thought of pouring the rest of her coffee into the sink. She had drunk almost all of it.

Then suddenly she remembered what Cheryl had said,

33

what the doctor had said, about the bitter taste. She tried to push her cup away and call to Cheryl, but everything seemed to be sliding downhill. She couldn't catch her breath. The room turned into a black, swirling haze, framing Cheryl's face as she came back from the living room. Marylou felt herself slipping from the chair.

They heard the siren again. Theresa had been sitting on the living room couch, staring into space. The sound of the siren roused her. She went to the kitchen, lifted a corner of the curtain, and looked out.

She saw the ambulance pull up to the Freaneys' house and stop. It was almost like some ghastly replay, except that this was daylight. A sunny morning.

Brian went over to her and put his arm around her waist. She didn't flinch, but she didn't feel anything for him. She was stone, cold dead.

They watched, neither of them moving. A few minutes later a stretcher was carried out and down the steps from the sun deck. Something must have happened to Cheryl. Then they saw her hovering in the doorway. Maybe it was Bonnie Ann. Or Mark. And more poisoned candy.

Brian mumbled an exclamation. Theresa watched it all impersonally, as though it were happening on a movie screen.

Cheryl looked up and saw them at the window. For a moment she seemed riveted, and then she turned away.

A police car arrived before the ambulance left. A uniformed trooper and the same investigator who had visited them earlier got out of it and went into the Freaneys' house. The ambulance drove away. Along the road, people stood in clusters, watching it.

When Theresa left the window, Brian pulled open the curtain, letting in a flood of morning sunshine. It was the first time Theresa had ever wanted the curtains closed in the daytime. She couldn't face the sunlight, and she did not want people to see her.

Brian said, "I wish we knew what that was all about."

"What difference does it make?" she asked. "Even if you know what happened, it's not going to make any difference."

He opened the curtains on all three kitchen windows. People were going in and out of Cheryl's house. Someone was carrying a small child.

Theresa asked, "Do you think it hurt?"

He turned from the window. It took him a moment to grasp what she was talking about. Then he said, "I think it was too quick. They said it was very quick."

The telephone rang. It was his mother, whom he had called last night from the hospital. He hadn't wanted to see her then. Or rather, he knew Theresa didn't want it. She didn't want to see anybody, but Marge Lonergan was determined to be with them now.

"I got somebody else to take my bus today," she said. "And Dad's off work. We'll be over in a little while. Do you need anything?"

"No." What they needed, they would never get. "We'll be here. Thanks."

He told Theresa they were coming. "She was their grandchild," he said. "They need to share it with us."

"It's okay."

"There'll probably be other people. It's just the sort of thing people do at a time like this."

"It's okay," she said again, and went to get dressed. She was combing her hair when someone knocked at the door. ✦

It was Jess Morehouse, the police investigator. He carried a clear, plastic bag with something wrapped inside it. Theresa wondered if it was Patty's trick-or-treat candy. Until that moment, she had not given a thought to Patty's trick-or-treat candy. Only to the piece that had killed her.

"I'm sorry to bother you again," Morehouse said, "but there's been another incident."

"Another?" Brian asked. "What do you mean?" He thought he knew what it meant, but it was so incredible that he rejected it.

"I mean someone else has collapsed with the same symptoms."

"One of the kids?"

"No, a young woman. She was having coffee with Mrs. Freaney."

Theresa stared, transfixed, at the plastic bag in his hand.

"Was it the candy?" she asked.

"We don't think so. They were drinking coffee. Mrs. Freaney was called to the telephone and left the young woman and her baby alone in the kitchen."

"Who was it?" Brian asked.

"A Marylou Grover." Morehouse held up the plastic bag. "I wouldn't have bothered you just now, but I'd like to ask you something important. Do you think there's any chance your daughter might have taken some of the sugar from this box?"

They couldn't really see the box, because it was wrapped. The colors seemed to be red and white. Theresa thought it might have been Red House brand.

"I don't see why. She had all that candy. But she did have a real sweet tooth." Theresa stopped, hearing her own words echo. She could not get used to talking about Patty in the past tense.

"It was found on the table," Morehouse said. "Mrs. Freaney can't remember where it was before that. She assumes it must have been in the cupboard."

"I don't think Patty would have taken it out of a cupboard," Theresa said. "She wasn't the kind to help herself in somebody else's home. Even a home she knew well."

37

Brian asked, "Didn't anybody see what she ate?"

"We don't know that yet. Mrs. Freaney was busy with another child at the time. I haven't had a chance to ask the children yet. Well . . ." Morehouse moved toward the door.

"How is Marylou? Mrs. Grover?" asked Brian.

"Hard to say. They took her to the hospital, of course." It was his own opinion, on the basis of what he saw, that Marylou Grover probably wasn't going to make it.

Later that day, investigators managed to track down the woman who had given out the Moon Bars. She was horrified when they told her about the needle. She had never done anything wrong, she said.

"I bought a string of them at the supermarket. You know, they were all packaged together, about a dozen, in a sort of strip. I didn't even take them off the strip until yesterday afternoon. I never looked at them. I didn't know."

She seemed to be telling the truth. They would follow it up, but it became a separate investigation when they were sure it had nothing to do with the Lonergan girl's death.

Meanwhile, the Freaneys' trash was being carefully sorted and analyzed. If Patty had succumbed to contaminated candy, there should have been a contaminated wrapper somewhere. If the candy had been unwrapped, then traces of cyanide would be found throughout her trick-or-treat bag. If nothing was found, it would be quite probable that she had ingested some of the sugar from the box on the table. That had been found to contain cyanide.

Just before noon, Brian's parents arrived, and with them, his sister-in-law Gwen.

Marge Lonergan asked in a discreet whisper, "When are you going to have the service?"

"Look, Mom," Brian said, "the police have been in and out of here all day. That's all we can deal with."

"But you have to start thinking about it," Marge persisted. "You can't just not think about it."

He realized that that was exactly what he wanted to do—not think about burying Patty.

He went to the bedroom, where Theresa had gone to retreat from his family. She was standing by the window, staring through the closed curtain.

He asked softly, "Honey, what do you want to do about the funeral?"

She didn't answer, but he knew she had heard him. And his mother was right. They couldn't put it off. Besides, it might be good for both of them in the long run. It would help them to pick up the pieces.

"I think we ought to go and make the arrangements," he said.

"You go."

"Don't you want anything to say about it?"

She shook her head. Marge and Gwen went with him. They helped him pick out a casket. Gwen ordered a blanket of flowers as a gift from Frank, Brian's brother, and herself. They went to the church and planned the day and time. Brian was asked what music he wanted. He couldn't think music. The others chose it for him.

They went back home and found two neighbors maintaining a vigil in the living room. Theresa was in the bedroom with the door closed. "She's lying down," one of the women explained.

Marge busied herself making coffee. People were bringing in food. Casseroles. Pasta dishes. Fancy desserts. The refrigerator couldn't hold it all.

More people arrived. His brother Frank. The families of the people he worked with at Reynolds Home Center. They all brought food.

When some of the people left, Theresa came out of her room. Marge made her eat a sandwich. Then she said, "Honey, we did all the arrangements for the service, but I thought we should leave it to you what you want her to wear."

Theresa sat still for a moment, and then looked up. "She died in that dress. And it meant a lot to her."

"The bride's costume?" Brian asked.

"It was the last thing I ever did for her," she said, "but I guess it's kind of chintzy. I don't know. I don't want to go in there and look at her clothes. I just don't want to go in her room."

Marge turned to Brian.

He said, "Maybe someday I could, but not now. And I don't know much about clothes."

"Maybe," Marge began, "maybe I could buy something for her. Something new. Would that be all right?"

Brian looked at Theresa. "I think that would be nice," he said. Although it sounded wasteful to him, and that made the whole thing again seem unreal.

Late in the afternoon Jess Morehouse knocked at the Lonergans' door to tell them about the sugar. It was definitely contaminated.

"We still don't know what else she might have eaten," he said, "but chances are good that she ingested some of that sugar, for whatever reason."

"I don't see why," Brian replied.

"Unfortunately, nobody noticed what she was eating," Jess went on. "Just before that, a little boy got hurt and they were all busy with him. We'll keep on checking, and we'll stay in touch."

"Yes," said Brian. Jess started down the steps.

"The Freaneys didn't know about the sugar?" Brian asked. Dumb question. But it was hard to be intelligent about a thing like that. He felt as if the whole mess was getting out of hand, like a giant, berserk snowball. "Who would—how did it get there?"

"That's what we're trying to find out," said Jess.

It changed everything, Brian thought. It wasn't any trick-or-treat candy. Maybe. They still couldn't be sure. But a box of cyanide right there on the kitchen table?

He put his hand to his forehead. He couldn't think. He didn't know whether it was the Freaneys, or whether they had been potential victims themselves. He didn't know anything except that his daughter was dead. Two people now. A pregnant young mother, too. Three, if you counted her baby. A box of poison right there on the table, and they had children in that house.

"Doesn't make sense, does it?" said Jess.

"Did you ask them?" A totally stupid question. He didn't know what made him say it.

"I asked the wife and kids. The husband isn't home yet. They say they don't know anything about it." Jess sympathized with the guy, but he couldn't talk about his investigation. "We'll keep in touch," he said again, and went back to his car.

Brian closed the door. He went over to Theresa, who sat by herself in a corner of the sofa, while Marge and Gwen ran the household.

"They think it was the sugar," he said. "They found cyanide in the sugar. And Marylou Grover is dead."

On the pretext of pouring himself more coffee, he went to the kitchen and looked out of the window at the Freaneys' house.

He couldn't understand it. A box of poisoned sugar. He just couldn't understand it.

Two miles away in Pine Glen, an elderly widow brewed herself a cup of tea.

Elizabeth Cardo lived alone in a small, dark house set against the side of a mountain. The mountain cut off the western sunshine, but Elizabeth turned on the light in her snug kitchen, pulled her wheelchair over to the dinette table, and took the tea bag from her tea. She stirred in two spoonfuls of sugar and let it cool for a minute or two.

The tea had a bitter taste. She couldn't really tell what was wrong. Her nose wasn't so good any more. Maybe she had made it too strong.

But you couldn't waste a good tea bag and all that sugar, and she needed the warmth. She drank the rest of it and waited for the satisfying glow to spread itself through her body.

7

Brian woke in the morning with a clear recollection of his pain. He wondered how many mornings he would have to wake with that pain. Common sense told him that eventually it would dull, and perhaps someday become only a background feeling, but he found that hard to believe.

Theresa lay beside him. He didn't think she was really asleep. Only pretending. She did not want him to touch her. As a small child, she hadn't had much physical affection. Her response in a crisis was to withdraw.

He went to the kitchen, which had been left clean and shining by all the people who were there yesterday. He opened the curtains, fixed himself a cup of instant coffee, and stood at the counter, drinking it. He saw Leonard Freaney come out of his house and get into his car. Cheryl stood on the sun deck to see him off. As Leonard backed out of the driveway, Cheryl looked up and gave a little start when she saw Brian watching her.

Can't keep her eyes off this house, he thought.

He swallowed the rest of his coffee and went to get dressed. Theresa's face was turned to the wall. If she hadn't been breathing, he might have thought she was dead. He pulled on his clothes, shaved, and went outside. Alice, left behind, scratched on the door. "Later," he called to her. "Hang in

there." He looked up at the sun shining above the pine trees.
The world goes on, he thought incredulously.

Cheryl answered his knock at once. He didn't miss her look
of consternation or her breathless apology. "Oh, Brian, I've
been meaning to come over—"

"That's okay." He was glad she hadn't. He edged past her
into the kitchen.

Young Mark, still in pajamas, was sitting at the table.
Cheryl seemed embarrassed at having him there. "He wasn't
feeling good today. I told him he could stay home from
school."

Mark looked up at their visitor and muttered a gruff "H'lo."

Cheryl fluttered nervously. She was edgy about something.
Brian wished he knew what it was. He said, "I just wanted to
find out some things."

"Well." She flapped her hands in a gesture of resigned
welcome. "Ask me anything you want."

He glanced at Mark, who sat contemplating a bowl of cold
cereal. Brian hadn't planned on having him there. It was
easier to talk to Cheryl alone. Mark would understand immediately what it was all about. He was too smart.

Mark's spoon clicked against the side of the dish.

"You can wash that when you're finished," Cheryl told him.
"I've already done my dishes." She explained to Brian, "He
had to wait in his room till Leonard left. If Leonard sees the
kids staying home from school, there's hell to pay."

"Yeah," added Mark, "especially for me. Once I had a fever
of a hundred four—"

Cheryl gave an impatient click of her tongue.

"I passed out in school," Mark went on. "When Dad heard
about it, he called me a fag, but it was his fault."

"Okay, Mark," said his mother.

"He's always calling me a fag. Did you hear about that
time he made me go hunting, Mr. Lonergan? I hate hunting."

"That's enough, Mark," Cheryl said again. "That was a

44

whole year ago, and it doesn't concern people outside the family."

Mark said, "By the way, Mr. Lonergan, I'm really sorry about—you know. About what happened."

"Yes. Thanks."

"I guess I didn't say that right. I shouldn't have said 'by the way.' It makes it sound incidental, and it's not."

Cheryl's impatience was clearly audible. "Shut up, Mark. You're running on." She started toward the living room. Brian followed her.

"She was a nice kid," Mark called after them, and Brian looked back at him gratefully.

Cheryl sat down on the sofa. She offered him coffee. Brian declined, and took a seat in an armchair. He regretted it immediately. It was Leonard's favorite chair and it had a feel of Leonard in it.

"I don't mean to bother you," he said. "I just wanted to find out some things for myself."

"The police already asked me all about it, you know."

"That's the police. I want to know for myself."

"I guess I'd feel the same way," she said uncertainly. "But you know, this is almost as hard for me as it is for you. I guess you don't believe that, but I feel—I mean, I just honestly can't figure out how it got there."

"The poison? Or the sugar?"

She looked bewildered. "The poison. I don't know."

"How long did you have the sugar?"

"That box? I just got it."

"Where?"

"The police already asked me all this, Brian."

"I told you, I want to know for myself. And you owe it to me." Because it was her house. Somebody had to owe him something. Apparently it hadn't occurred to her that the police might not share their information with the victim's family.

She sighed. "Okay. At the Pine Glen Market." The only

45

grocery store in the village. "Usually I go to Shop Rite in Valley Center, but I always forget things and then I stop in at the market. It's so sad—"

She faltered under his steady gaze. He supposed it was hard for her, but he didn't really care.

"I wonder if it could have been poisoned after it got here," he said.

"That's ridiculous! That would mean—well, that's what they thought at first, but why would anybody—"

"Why would anybody anyway?"

"I just don't know." Her hands opened and closed. "I don't know why any of it happened. How could I?"

"You have to understand how it looks," he said. "The poison was in your house, and two people have already died. And neither of them were members of your family."

She raised her chin and glared at him. "What's that supposed to mean? You think we had anything to do with it? That's crazy, Brian. And what about the one last night?"

"What one last night?"

"Didn't you listen to the radio? Some old woman in the village. They found her this morning. The neighbors saw her lights on all night. And there was a box of sugar on the table. Same brand."

Another box of sugar? Then it wasn't just the Freaneys? He couldn't believe it.

"It makes a difference, doesn't it?" she said gently.

He didn't want it to make a difference. He wanted to be angry. At someone. And not someone faceless and abstract.

He stood up. "Thanks for your time."

"Oh, it's nothing, Brian."

She was gushing. He thought she still felt vaguely guilty, and he was glad. Somebody should.

He did not look at Mark as he went out. He wished he had known about the other victim before she told him. He crossed the road to his own home and called Jess Morehouse.

46

Jess sounded weary. "Yeah," he said, "Elizabeth Cardo. Her daughter works at the restaurant where I had lunch yesterday. The poor woman was in a wheelchair."

Elizabeth Cardo. He had known her slightly in the past. He knew her daughter Jennie a little better.

At least she had a life, he thought bitterly.

"The funeral's tomorrow," he told Jess. "Two o'clock."

"Right."

"Was it the sugar? With Mrs. Cardo?"

"Looks that way. We haven't got a report yet."

"You say she was in a wheelchair. How did she get her groceries?"

"A neighbor shopped for her yesterday. Look, Brian—"

"Where?"

"Brian, we're working on this thing, believe me. They called me out of bed this morning. I just got back from Cardo's house, just before you called."

"Why'd they get you out of bed?"

"Because of the sugar, okay? I'll see you tomorrow. Sooner, if I have anything."

Tomorrow, at the funeral. Jess would be there, watching to see who came. It probably wouldn't do any good. A killer who didn't need to see his victims die, who apparently didn't even care who they were, probably wouldn't need to see them buried.

The day of Patty's funeral was mild and sunny, with a soft haze in the air. Gone was the sharpness of that Halloween night. It felt more like September than early November. When Theresa and Brian and their relatives and friends returned to the trailer afterward, the children of the park were all outside, playing on their bicycles, their roller skates, and toy motorcycles.

Brian saw the way Theresa looked at them as he parked the car. He remembered all the summer afternoons when he had

47

come home from work and Patty had been there too, on her bike.

That bike was still out in back, by the storage shed. He had wondered what to do with it. Maybe he would leave it right where it was, as a kind of monument to his grief, so that everyone could see it rusting away, season after season.

"They don't seem to care," Theresa said. "Even Bonnie Ann. She didn't go to the funeral."

"No, uh—Cheryl didn't want the kids to go. She thought it would be morbid."

"She told you that?"

"Yes. She hoped I'd understand."

"Did you?"

"No."

They got out of the car and went into their house. Other cars came and parked in the ditch along the roadway. The children, riding by, looked curiously at the people going into the Lonergans' trailer. They knew why they were there. Only Gus Bova, in a suit and tie, had attended the funeral with his mother. Ann Bova joined the guests at the Lonergans', but Gus changed into his jeans and went out to play.

It made sense, Brian admitted. There were no other kids at this occasion, whatever it was called. Not a wake. This was after. A party? That didn't sound right, even though eating seemed to be the purpose of it. Marge and Gwen had brought food from a deli caterer in Valley Center and were hauling it out of the refrigerator and setting up a buffet. There were not enough places for people to sit and most of them stood, eating from plastic plates and talking with one another like a cocktail party. He knew it was hard on Theresa, having so many people around acting relatively cheerful, but you couldn't tell them to go away.

A woman came up to him and introduced himself as Patty's teacher. And Ann Bova talked about what had happened to Gus with the needle, and clutched Brian's arm, saying over and over again how she wished it could have been just a thing

48

like that with Patty. She meant it, too. Jess Morehouse stood watching everyone and finding nothing. They were all family, friends, and neighbors.

After a while they began to leave. Marge and Gwen and some of the others cleaned up the remnants of the feast, and then they left, too. It was only Brian and Theresa in their empty house.

Now, he thought, it's over. Now we're supposed to take a deep breath and get on with the rest of our lives.

Theresa sat on the sofa with Alice's head in her lap. Alice looked up at her as though wanting an explanation for all that had happened.

Theresa stroked the golden fur. "I don't understand it, either," she told the dog. "I just don't understand. Why us?" She looked at Brian. "Of all the things that could happen—"

The police had found, in Patty's trick-or-treat bag, one opened package of candy. It was a set of three fruit jellies in the shape of flowers. They were called Daisy Treats. When the package was complete, there would have been a green one, a red one, and a yellow one. The green one was missing. A little girl who had been at the Freaneys' that night reported that Patty had made a comment about lime candy. Yes, Theresa had agreed, Patty was crazy about lime. Lime pies, sour balls, anything. But why the sugar?

The police had bought Daisy Treats and tasted them. The lime and the lemon ones were tart. Maybe too tart for a kid who loved sweets. They conjectured that she might have tried to improve it with some of the sugar from the tainted box. It was only a theory, but the autopsy results were consistent with it.

"Why?" Theresa cried. "Why did she have to take that piece of candy in the Freaneys' kitchen?"

"Because she liked lime," he said.

It was all a matter of chance. That Patty had chosen the lime to eat first when most children would have grabbed for chocolate. That she had put sugar on it—if she had—instead of

49

throwing it out when she found it too tart. That the box of sugar conveniently at hand happened to be laced with cyanide. That Cheryl had purchased that particular box of sugar—unless they were all poisoned.

The only thing that wasn't chance was the poisoning itself. It seemed nearly impossible that the sugar could have been accidentally contaminated. Investigators had already traced the chain of refining, packaging, and distribution. Cyanide played no part in it. Someone deliberately, and with malice aforethought, had mixed that cyanide into the sugar.

She was in the dark room. And now she knew she had been there forever. She had never gotten out of it.

She hugged herself tightly so the spiders would not get on her from the basement walls. She couldn't smell the basement. But she could feel—something.

And then she heard it. A voice. And she smelled cigarette smoke.

"Who are you?" she asked. "Where am I?"

"Never mind," said the voice.

"Who are you? Why are you here?"

She was very cold. She hugged herself and shivered because she was cold.

The voice said, "He thinks you don't remember."

She didn't know whether it was talking to her. "Remember what?"

"Don't remember what he did to you."

She didn't remember what anyone had done. She had been in the dark room all her life.

"Tell me," she begged, "what's happening. I don't understand."

She thought the voice had gone away. Then it said, "You don't remember when they buried you."

She was Patty!

She fought against the sand on her face, in her mouth, her nose. She struggled to breathe, to fight her way out.

"Theresa!" That was a voice she knew. "My God, honey, what is it?"

She opened her eyes and saw Brian in the gray morning light.

"Patty," she gasped. "She can't breathe. I felt her. She's alive!"

"No, honey, it's not like that. You just want her to be alive. So do I, but it's over."

He was in bed and she lay beside him on top of the blankets. Her feet were cold. She tried to sit up.

"What are you doing out of bed?" He tugged at the blankets, trying to pull them out from under her and put them over her.

"It was a dream," she said.

"I know. It must have been a bad one."

"I was in a dark room. Where Mrs. Sentry used to put me. But there was somebody else."

"You're awake now. It's okay."

"I heard a voice. It talked to me. I didn't know who it was. It said something about burying me. And then I felt as if I was being buried and it made me think of Patty."

She had to get off the bed, even if she was cold. She had to know.

"Where are you going?" he called as she ran to the living room.

She turned on the lamp beside the sofa and looked in the ashtray. Her heart pounded when she heard him coming. He mustn't see—

The ashtray was empty. She put her hand to her chest.

Empty, but there were a few drops of water.

He took her in his arms and held her closely. She was shivering from the cold. "Listen, honey," he said.

"I don't want to talk about it."

"What did you come bolting out here for?"

52

"I just wanted to check on something."

"On what? Tell me. What's the matter?"

"Never mind."

That was what the voice had said. "Never mind."

"Listen, I know you're upset. It's only natural," he said as he led her back to bed. "But it's running you ragged. Maybe if you went to see a doctor—"

"I don't need a doctor. I just need Patty. You're trying to say I'm sick. I have a pretty good reason for feeling this way."

"Of course you have. I didn't say you were sick. I just thought maybe they could help you deal with it. Maybe give you a tranquilizer, or something."

"I don't want chemicals. I want my child."

"Well . . ." He eased her into the bed and then went around to his own side.

"Neither of us wants it to be real," he said, lying with his hands under his head. "I guess it'll take a while before we can really accept it. In the meantime, I don't think there's anything wrong with asking for some help. There's no reason why we have to punish ourselves. We've been punished enough. And for what?"

"You can take pills if you want them," she murmured into the pillow. "I don't want them."

He lay on his back, staring up at the darkness. He couldn't help her. He could only help himself. Maybe he was just as sick as she was in his obsession with finding the killer, but he thought it made a little more sense. It was possible and necessary to find the killer, but it wasn't possible to wish Patty back to life.

At nine-thirty that morning he entered the Pine Glen Market. Dorian Baxter looked up from the cash register with a tentative half smile. He was getting used to those smiles. People didn't know how to take him any more. And he hadn't been in here, hadn't seen Dorian, in how long?

She finished checking out a customer and then turned to

53

him. There was a soft light in her large, aquamarine eyes.

"Hi, Brian." Her voice was low and creamy. He remembered how it used to excite him. Everything about her had excited him once.

"Oh, baby." She reached across the counter and seized his hand. "I don't know what to say, it's just too horrible. I can't believe it would happen. You're such a sweet guy."

"Yeah," he said, trying tactfully to disentangle himself.

She looked embarrassed and perhaps a little miffed, but quickly overcame it. "How's Theresa holding up?"

"Not so good."

"The poor thing. Her only child."

"Mine, too," he said.

"Well, uh—yes. For both of you, it's just awful."

He looked around the store. It was deserted. He had never seen it that way before. There were always a few people browsing up and down the aisles. Even the arcade games in the back corner were quiet. He couldn't believe that.

"Not so good, is it?" he said.

"No, I have to tell you, it's pretty bad. People found out both boxes came from here."

"Do you think it might be anything against the store?"

"I honestly don't know. The police already asked about that. I couldn't think of any reason, but you never know what somebody's going to build up in their mind. Anyhow, that's one of the first things they thought of. They've been checking into Red House employees, too, you know. Everything."

"So they've already looked the place over."

"You'd better believe it. And they took away all the Red House sugar."

"Find anything?"

"Not that I know of."

"I mean in the other boxes of sugar."

A truck driver came into the store and bought a pack of cigarettes. When he left, Brian asked, "How would anybody get into it and then make it look as if they hadn't? There's a tear strip, isn't there?

"I guess if you were careful you could undo one of the end flaps and then glue it shut again. I never really looked at those boxes, and I don't have any left to show you."

"Do you remember who bought them?"

"Huh?"

"Who might have bought them and then returned them to the shelf?"

"Oh, for heaven's sake, do you think I notice things like that? It might look empty now, but a lot of people come in here. Kids, old people, men, women. Do you think I keep a list of who buys what? And if they wanted to put something back, I wouldn't know. It's way over there, out of my sight."

"I realize that. I was just asking."

"Aw, Brian, I'm sorry." She reached for his hand again and massaged his knuckle with her thumb. "It's just that—I was going to say it's just that this whole thing is getting to me, but nothing like what it's doing to you."

"It's my whole life," he said.

"Yes, I know how it is for you. I have a kid, too, you know. Sometime, when you have a chance, I wish you'd come over and see my kid. Come and see both of us, I mean."

She had always been after him. They had had a thing going once years ago, after he got back from Vietnam. Then she had run off to the city and he met Theresa, and that was that. But since then, she had made it quite clear that if he and Theresa ever split up, Dorian would be available.

"Maybe I will sometime," he said, to keep the peace. "How are things going with you?"

She sighed. "What a guy, asking about me at a time like this. We're okay. Cliffie's okay. He—"

"What have you been doing with yourself?"

"Same as always. Running the store. Going home to Cliffie. I see Hank Aiken now and then. Remember Hank? He never gives up on me. Wait a minute, I just thought of something. Remember you asked if it could be anything against the store? Well, I got to thinking, you know Hank has this thing for me. He's getting a paunch already, Brian, and he's thinning on top. It makes him desperate, know what I mean? That kind of intensity, it's such a turn-off. Just a couple of weeks ago he asked me again and I said no. Well, you can't help wondering."

"If Hank might have done it?" Brian was genuinely surprised.

"He's always been a little weird, hasn't he?"

"You'd have to be more than a little weird to do a thing like that," he said. He was thinking. Henry Aiken . . .

"Okay, it's just an idea I had. If you told me to name somebody, he's the only one I could come up with. Do you think I should tell the police?"

"No. It's too far out."

"Don't forget, I own a third of this store. If he wanted to get back at me—" She turned to watch as a pair of teenagers came in. They went straight to the back corner. A moment later one of the arcade games beeped into action.

"Well, that's something, anyway," she said. "It makes the place sound alive. Anyhow, Brian, the police already went through all this. Everything I've told you, except about Hank. But don't get me wrong, I'm glad you came in."

"I'm aware," he said, "that the police are doing their job, but I have to know these things for myself."

"Well, I don't blame you, but I kind of think you're just aggravating yourself."

"Maybe. But it gives me something to do."

"Yeah, you're right. If I think of anything else, I'll let you know. And do come over sometime. Cliffie and I would love to see you."

"Sure," he said as he left the store. It wasn't Cliffie who wanted to see one of his mother's old boyfriends. Dorian had gone to the city to try a modeling career, and instead had come home with Cliffie. She said she had been married briefly. Everyone pretended to believe her because it was the polite thing to do. And maybe it was true.

He wondered what he should do about Henry Aiken. There was so little to go on. If anyone mentioned him to the police, it should be Dorian. But Henry was an old acquaintance of his. They had gone all the way through school together. There was no reason why he couldn't approach the man himself.

Theresa woke to the smell of cigarettes. From the light, she could tell it was late in the morning. She looked at the clock. Eleven-thirty. And Brian wasn't there.

She sat up, pressing a hand to the side of her head. She had never slept so late.

Again she smelled the smoke. Maybe Brian had a guest. But then he would have closed the bedroom door to give her privacy. She listened for a moment, heard only silence, and went out to the living room. He was gone, and the front door was locked.

He hadn't gone to work. She wasn't sure what day it was, but thought it was the weekend.

Still, someone had been there. The ashtray was full. She emptied it into the toilet. She turned on the kitchen and bathroom exhaust fans to air out the smell. It might have been someone visiting Brian, but she couldn't be sure. She did not want him to know.

One of the dining chairs had been moved across the room and placed next to the telephone. He had sat there talking to somebody. Maybe his mother. Or maybe Cheryl, or that woman at the store. He got along so well with women. Or maybe the police investigator.

"I hate this," she said aloud. "I hate not knowing."

Somewhere in the room, someone laughed.

"Where are you?"

Again there was silence. It had been in her head. She was going crazy. Really crazy.

Maybe if she had some coffee. Or tea. She filled the kettle with water and tried to turn on a burner. Then she could smell the gas. The pilot light was out.

She reached for the matches, but they were not on the shelf where they belonged. Whoever had been smoking must have taken them.

She began opening drawers and looking on other shelves. There had to be matches somewhere. They always had matches. She left the exhaust fan on to pipe out the gas. She didn't think it was dangerous, not for a while, but she hated the smell. Mobile homes were too well insulated. The gas could accumulate.

She pulled open a drawer in the dining room buffet. There were place mats and candles and—

Two calico potholders, one red and one yellow. A birthday gift from Patty, who had made them herself.

"No," she whimpered as she picked them up and held them to her face.

When Brian came home he found her slumped in a chair by the telephone, crying.

"She made these for me," Theresa sobbed. "I just found them in a drawer. She made them for my birthday, and I was saving them."

"What are they?" he asked.

She handed him one, a red, quilted potholder soaked with her tears. He didn't know what to do. He wished he could help her, but there was no way to change things.

He looked down at the potholder Theresa had given him. Someone must have helped Patty use the sewing machine. God, there would be years of this.

Finally Theresa quieted and sat exhausted, staring at the floor.

"I wish it was something else," she said. "If something had

to happen, I wish it was your job, or mine. Or the house burning down. But that wouldn't work, because we have insurance. It wouldn't be bad enough."

"Do you really think we're being punished?" he asked. "For what?"

"I don't know."

He knew she didn't know. She had never known. As a child, she had been mistreated. Children like that, he had learned, tended to grow up believing that they must somehow deserve it. He didn't think she was really aware of feeling that way. He could see it more than she could, because someone had explained it to him once.

And now this. It would be terrible for anybody, but it was enough to kill Theresa. She deserved something good in her life. More than just eight years of Patty.

"Honey," he said, "life isn't meant to be a system of rewards and punishments. It just isn't meant to be fair."

"Why isn't it?"

"I don't mean it's supposed to be unfair, but it just doesn't work out all nice and neat. That's what I'm saying. And don't ask me how you're supposed to deal with it being like that, because I don't know either."

She thought about it for a while. Then she asked, "Where were you just now?"

"At the Market. I went in to ask about the sugar."

"Was that girl there?"

"Dorian? Yes, she was there."

"What did she say?"

"She said the police already asked her. I figured they did, but that wasn't the point. I'm not doing it for them. She said they took all the Red House sugar. And there was hardly anybody there. Business has really fallen off. So maybe—"

She turned away. She didn't want to hear any more.

"Look," he said, "whatever they find, whatever the reason they turn up, it's not going to make any sense. We have to face that. There's just no sense to what happened. Whatever somebody's problem is, it had nothing to do with Patty.

There's no damn reason in the world why she has to be dead, so there's no point in looking for one."

Theresa studied the yellow potholder in her hand. "Sometimes," she said, "I get angry at the Freaneys."

"Do you think I don't?"

"I know it's not fair."

"I even told her that," he said. "I told Cheryl there are two people dead because of poison in her house, and not one of the Freaneys even has a scratch."

"What did she say?"

"She got pissed. As if I was telling her it ought to be them who were hurt. And maybe I was. Look, I'm going to call a friend of mine, a guy I knew in school."

"Is that why you had the chair out here?" she asked.

"I didn't have the chair out here. I thought you pulled it out."

They looked at each other. Theresa was the first to turn away. Again he thought what a terrible strain she was under. And that must bother her, too, knowing she wasn't herself. He could see that she was bothered about the chair, blowing it all out of proportion.

He dialed Henry Aiken's number. He hardly knew what to say, but Henry did not sound surprised to hear from him.

"There's something I'd like to see you about," Brian said. "Are you going to be around in half an hour?"

"Around here? Sure. Are you coming to my house?"

He didn't ask why Brian wanted to see him. He didn't mention Patty, although it had been prominent in the newspapers for several days.

"I'm going up to Valley Center," Brian told his wife. "I'll be back in a little while, okay? Theresa?"

"Okay." She did not even bother to look up as he left. He felt her deadness inside himself as he drove to Valley Center. He wondered if either of them would ever be able to live again.

Henry Aiken was outside clearing the leaves from his lawn. He had a lawn vacuum cleaner with a big red bag.

61

"What do you do with it when it gets full?" Brian asked after Henry switched it off.

"I fill up about half a dozen trash bags, then I take them to the woods and dump them," Henry answered.

"In your car? Isn't that a lot of trouble?"

"What do you do?"

"I don't know," Brian said, not because he didn't know, but because it didn't seem important.

"Did you know I lost my daughter?" he asked.

Henry looked as though he had been struck. Then he said, "Yes," and his face went red. He began to babble. "I saw it in the paper. And when I saw it was you, I just—I didn't—I was going to call you. No. Write a note. I was going to write a note."

"That's okay, I know it embarrasses people. I'm getting used to it."

"No, it isn't that."

"That's exactly what it is. Don't think I don't know. I'd probably feel the same way. People don't know what to say, so they avoid you."

It wasn't going right. He hadn't come here to reassure Henry.

"I lost my daughter," he said, "because some fruitcake poisoned the sugar in the Pine Glen Market." He paused, watching carefully. "You go in there a lot to see Dorian."

Again Henry's face turned a dull red. "Not a lot."

"I just wondered if you might have noticed anything."

"If I did, I'd report it, wouldn't I?"

Henry's discomfort had gone. He was truculent. It could have meant something, or nothing.

"You wouldn't necessarily," Brian said. "If you saw somebody messing with the sugar, you wouldn't think anything about it, till afterward when something happened."

Henry pursed his lips and stared at his shoe. They were sitting in the living room of his small, old-fashioned house. It had a faint musty odor, as though it had been closed for a long time. It hadn't been closed; it only smelled that way. Henry sat sprawled in an armchair with his legs projected straight in front of him. He twisted his foot back and forth, examining the shoe.

"When did you change careers, Bri?" he asked.

"I don't have a career. Just a job."

"I mean, coming around with all these questions."

"I know what you mean. I didn't. Nothing's changed, except that I lost my daughter."

Henry flinched. It was the second time he had reacted that way. Anyone who didn't know him, Brian reflected, might be led to think there was something on his mind. But as far as he knew, there had never been anything on Henry's mind.

"Terrible shame about your daughter," Henry said gruffly.

"More than you know."

"Don't rub it in, Bri."

"Don't rub what in?"

"That you have kids and I don't."

"That I—have—kids?"

"Never mind."

"What are you talking about, Henry?"

Henry raised his voice. "Never mind! That wasn't meant the way it sounds."

Brian would have left it there, except for Henry's strange behavior. "Then how was it meant? Tell me. You know I only had one kid and she's gone, so we're even now, if that's what you want."

"Jesus, you know I didn't mean that. It's just—hell, you said you went to see Dorian."

"I only went in today to ask her about the sugar. Otherwise I hardly ever see Dorian."

"Wish I could believe that," Henry muttered.

"You can."

"She didn't tell you anything?"

"Nothing. You're right, I shouldn't be doing this. I've gone a little crazy. It can happen, you know. She was our only

63

child. Even if she weren't, it's hard just to sit back and take it." Brian stood up to leave.

Henry pulled in his feet and hoisted himself from the chair. "You sure she didn't tell you anything?"

"What did you have in mind, exactly?"

"Nothing to do with your daughter. I'm sorry."

"What should she tell me, Henry?"

"Forget it. It's nothing to do with your daughter."

"With what? The sugar?"

"Not with any of this. I'm sorry. I shouldn't have said anything."

Brian reached for the man's shirt, grabbing a handful of it at the open neck. "What?"

"Nothing. Nothing. Stop it, you're choking me!"

"*What?*"

"I told you, it's not what you think. And I'd appreciate it if you keep away from Dorian."

Brian let go of the shirt. "Anything to oblige, Henry."

"I mean it. Stay away from her. You've got a woman of your own."

"So that's it. You're policing the public morals. How admirable, Henry." Brian headed toward the door. He needed to think about this. Henry had almost told him something and it was making him crazy.

But in the car he decided that Henry was the one who was crazy. Always had been, and now he was off his rocker with jealousy, too.

Was he crazy enough to have poisoned the sugar in Dorian's store? Maybe he wanted to drive her out of business so she would have to marry him for security.

Not Dorian, he concluded. She could always take care of herself, and Henry would know it. It was only a wild possibility. He had reached the point where he was grasping for any sort of answer.

He had to stop thinking about it. Somehow he had gotten out of Aiken's house with his composure intact, but as he drove home, the whole thing bubbled up in his mind. He thought he understood the significance of what Henry was trying to tell him. Whether or not it was true, he couldn't tell.

It didn't make sense. How would Henry know, when Dorian had never said anything? She wouldn't have told Henry and not Brian.

Just today she had begged him to come over and see Cliffie. It would mean so much to Cliffie, she had said. And there was something else, but he couldn't remember it.

He tried to call up a picture of Cliffie. Was there any possibility? Any resemblance? Maybe he would have to go over there and find out.

It was no wonder that she never seemed to let go of him, in spite of Theresa. And that had been only since her return from New York with Cliffie. Before that, when he had thought briefly that he might want to marry her, she hadn't been interested. She had wanted to go to New York and break into modeling. She said she owed it to herself at least to try. He hadn't really thought she'd make it. Apart from those eyes, her face was quite ordinary. And that wasn't the only strike against her. If what Henry said was true, she had been pregnant before she even got there.

It was only Henry's word. And Henry had always been jealous of him because of Dorian. Still, if it ever got back to Theresa, she would be devastated. Even more than she already was, if that was possible. He wondered if she had reached her saturation point.

He arrived at home to find Theresa dressed, but still in her hollow-eyed lethargy. The bed was unmade and the dining chair that had been pulled out by the telephone was still there.

"The policeman called," she said.

"Who, Jess?"

"Whatever his name is. He said they found another box at the Pine Glen Market."

She sounded as though she didn't care. All that mattered was the past. Now her life was over. He watched her for a moment, helplessly. There was nothing he could do for her, and he had to know what was going on. He picked up the phone and called Jess.

"Right," said Jess. "The third one at that little store. We figure it might be somebody who has it in for the store."

"Did you talk to Dorian Baxter?" Brian asked.

"Yeah, we did."

"And?"

"Nothing."

"She told me something."

"Yeah?"

"She has what they call a rejected suitor. I just talked to him."

There was a pause. Then Jess said, "Would you go over that again, please?"

Brian went over it again, telling Jess about his interviews with Dorian and Henry. He left out the part about Dorian's son.

Jess sighed. "I wish you could have persuaded Miss Baxter to come to us."

"She said she just thought of it," Brian explained. "And I know what you're thinking. You want me to butt out."

66

"Do you know why?" Jess exploded. "What if this Aiken character does know something? Now you've warned him, scared him off before we could even get to him. You're obstructing an official investigation, buddy."

"I thought of that. I guess I'm too wound up."

"Well, unwind. God's sake, do you want to blow this whole thing? Don't you want us to catch the guy?"

"I want me to catch the guy," Brian replied.

"You could end up letting him slip right through. You don't want that any more than we do. I know what this is like. I can't come down too hard on you, but will you do yourself a favor? Just relax and let us handle it. It's our job and we're trained for it."

"Sure it's your job. But the creep is mine, not yours."

"That's not the way it works, Lonergan. In a criminal case, it's the people versus the creep. And I am an investigating officer employed by the people of New York State. Even if you were permitted to handle it yourself, he's not yours alone. Not any more. What about the husband of that pregnant girl? What about the old lady's daughter?"

"I know. I know them both better than you do. How they deal with their loss is up to them. Now tell me about the sugar you found."

Jess Morehouse grumbled some more and then told him. It was one of the boxes they found on the shelf at the store. The front flap had been glued shut, almost as Dorian had suggested. For a moment, Brian found himself wondering about Dorian, but he put it out of his mind. It was something anybody could have thought of.

He thanked Jess for having called.

"Just want you to know we're on the case," Jess muttered.

"I guess that means there's no real target," Brian said. "Nobody in particular."

"Completely random," agreed Jess. "A mad bomber sort of thing."

"Is there anybody that crazy around Pine Glen?"

"We're looking. You never can tell."

He didn't care if the tragedy had gone beyond his family. He still wanted the person who did it. Maybe more than ever. It was all so stupid and senseless.

He hung up the phone and punched his fist into his hand.

"I know," said Theresa, misunderstanding his anger. "I wanted to hate the Freaneys."

"Did you?" He remembered that they had talked about it. He felt the same way.

"It's easier. At least we know who they are," she said.

"And none of them died."

"If it's somebody who did it completely at random, how are you ever going to find him?"

"I don't know. But I'm going to. Before the police."

"Don't you think—" She stopped and tried again. "I don't think it's right. It doesn't feel right, that kind of attitude. Not for Patty. It's too violent."

"It's not for Patty," he said, "it's for us. All right, for me. For the way I feel. And what about the violence against her?"

"She was so sweet. And we liked her that way."

"That's fine for Patty. That was back in a better world."

At least for a while it had been a better world. But before that, they had both known the irrationality of violence, she from her childhood, he from Vietnam. Maybe it was Patty who had made the difference.

Still, he couldn't help the way he felt.

Theresa remained lost in thought. He knew she was a non-violent person, not out of conviction, perhaps, but fear. An abused child. Where had all the anger gone? You couldn't be treated like that and not build up a lot of anger. She must have buried it under layers of fear. She would not have dared show anger to Mrs. Sentry and the others. That would only have brought down more violence.

She raised her head. "I have something to tell you. I hope you don't mind."

"I don't mind anything about you, honey." Except maybe her need to apologize for existing.

"While you were out, I called Nancy. I'm not going back to work."

"Okay," he said, "if that's what you want to do."

"Maybe later I'll look for something else, but I don't want to be around children."

"Is that all you have against Nancy?"

"For me, it's a lot. I just couldn't stand it."

Considering how she felt, he could see that the decision was right for her. But he wondered what she was going to do with herself all day.

"Maybe you ought to try to find something," he said. "Not for the money, but for you. It's not good to stay home alone and brood."

"But I don't want to go out in public. I'm not ready."

"Honey—"

"I mean it. I keep having blackouts. Sometimes I don't know what I'm doing. They'll think I'm crazy."

"Maybe you should—"

"And don't tell me to see a doctor."

"It's nothing to be afraid of."

"I'm not afraid. I'm just not interested." She went back to the bedroom and closed the door. Not out of anger at him, but because she couldn't face the world. He wondered if he would end up losing her, too.

It made him think again of Dorian and what Henry had implied. He didn't really believe it, but he found the idea intriguing. He would have liked to hear it from Dorian. If it was true.

And then?

He felt a mixture of excitement and frustration. Even if it were true, there wasn't much he could do about it. He couldn't have the child and he couldn't leave Theresa. He wouldn't want to leave her even if he felt he could. There wasn't anything he could do about the child, so what difference did it make?

Couldn't leave Theresa. But it would be one hell of a life if

Theresa went on the way she was. A hell of a bind. He didn't know what to do.

In this new light it made more sense, the way Dorian still played up to him after all these years. Maybe she only said the kid was his, maybe it really was. By the time she came back from New York with Cliff, he was married to Theresa. Then it was too late for Dorian, but that was when she seemed to decide she wanted him. And she never gave up.

He felt a sudden chill. What if, out of desperation—

No, she couldn't have. She would not have done the unthinkable. Not even for spite. Not to Patty.

He couldn't imagine anyone being so vicious. At least, not anybody he knew. And what about those other people who died? Would she have done that? A cover-up, maybe.

Then he remembered that the sugar had been in the Freaneys' house, that Patty had taken it—if she had—quite unexpectedly.

A random thing. That was all it was. The victims unwittingly chose themselves instead of the other way around.

In a way, he was glad when Monday came. Although he shared some of Theresa's aversion to a curious public, he was glad to be out of the house and busy again. The only trouble was, at the end of the day he would have to go back home. There would be no Patty, and Theresa, understandably, was hardly herself. He had left her in bed that morning. He hoped he wouldn't find her still there when he got home.

She heard the door close. She even heard him click the lock, to protect her while she was still in bed.

She sat up. Immediately she thought of the ashtray. Was it full again? What if he had seen it first?

She got out of bed and ran to the living room. The ashtray was empty and clean. She hoped he had found it that way and not cleaned it himself. She went to the kitchen window to make sure his car had gone.

The effort tired her. She stood at the counter, trying not to

70

give in and sit down. She would never be able to get through the rest of her life. And why should she have to?

For Brian, she thought.

She had really intended to get dressed that day. To make some kind of effort, but it scarcely seemed worthwhile.

Maybe if she had some coffee. But the thought of it revolted her. Maybe a drink. Just this once. She deserved it.

"No, it's not for you."

That voice again. And it wasn't in her head. It was a real voice, somewhere outside herself.

She looked out on the road in both directions. No one was there. The sound would not have carried into her house anyway, because the storm windows were up.

This was what it felt like to go crazy. The voice had sounded so real. She could have sworn it belonged to a real person.

"—back to bed."

"No," she answered. "Where are you? Tell me where you are."

It was Brian. Hiding. Playing tricks on her.

"Brian, where are you?"

"I'm Michael," said the voice.

"Who's Michael? I don't know any Michael."

Then she realized the danger. Her daughter had been murdered. And now this. It might even be the same person.

"Where are you?" she cried again. If somebody had been there, Alice would have barked. Instead, Alice was sleeping in a patch of sunshine under the living room windows.

"I'm right here."

"Where?"

"Right here, where you are."

"But you can't be!"

"Nothing you can do. Go back to bed. Sleep."

She stood where she was, feeling the throbbing in her brain. She wanted to go back to bed. She wanted to forget everything that had happened, but was afraid of what he might do if she were asleep.

71

Clutching the side of her head, she went to the bathroom and took two aspirins. The pain was so severe it squeezed her eyes closed. She forced them open, forced herself to get dressed. If she lay down for even a moment, she would be off her guard.

I'm crazy, she thought. I'm crazy.

She did not know which was worse: to be crazy, hearing voices in her head, or to have him be a real person. Either way, she was trapped, either inside or outside her head.

When she bent down to make the bed, her headache grew worse. She had wanted to keep busy, clean the place and surprise Brian. She couldn't do it. Not with this head. She gave up and lay down. She closed her eyes, keeping her head very still. As the headache faded away, she fell asleep.

She woke, hearing the telephone ring. She did not know how long it had been ringing, but as soon as she was awake, it stopped. She lay on the bed, staring at her feet. She was wearing shoes, her navy blue sneakers. She could not remember putting them on.

She thought back, trying to recall every detail of what she had done before falling asleep.

Michael. There was a voice named Michael. It was the same voice as always, but now it had a name.

She remembered thinking it was real, and not her imagination. That was the terrible part. Somebody right there, but hidden. Hidden where there was no place to hide.

It was my imagination, she thought, now that she could no longer hear it.

And that meant she was crazy, or getting there. She would have to watch herself. Not do anything strange or forgetful. She thought it might be all right, in her circumstances, to go a little crazy. It was better that way than if it were a real person, lurking and waiting. Someone who might have killed Patty. Who might have to kill again to protect himself.

The clock by her bedside said it was two in the afternoon.

The better part of the day had gone. If she kept this up, she could sleep away the rest of her life.

She sat up, realizing it was not only the telephone that had waked her. The house was very cold. She went out to the living room and looked at the thermostat. It was set at fifty-five degrees. She knew it hadn't been that cold before. Brian always pushed it up to sixty-eight in the morning.

She began to feel the fear again. The fear that someone was there, in the shadows. The fear . . .

Her car keys were in the middle of the dining table. The fear froze her now. She always kept them in her purse.

Maybe she was doing these things herself. But she had been asleep. She hadn't moved.

Except that she was wearing shoes. She never wore her street shoes in the house.

She couldn't tell Brian. Couldn't tell anyone. No one must know until she figured it out for herself.

11

The next morning, they heard it on the radio. The deaths had spread to Valley Center. A pair of shopkeepers, Charles and Renée Minkoff, had been found dead in the apartment over their small store, K & M Groceries. A married son and daughter, unable to reach them by phone, had gone over to investigate and found the bodies. Police had discovered an empty Red House sugar box in the garbage, and a small canister full of sugar which they were testing for cyanide.

Brian rushed into the bedroom. "Did you hear that?"

"Yes, I did," Theresa replied.

"Sorry. I didn't mean to have it so loud, and I forgot to close the door." He looked sheepish. It didn't matter. That was not what bothered her.

"I was getting up anyway," she said.

"You don't have to. You can rest as long as you want."

She wished he wouldn't treat her like an invalid.

She remembered the car keys. And her shoes.

"When did they buy the sugar?" she asked.

"Didn't say. Why?"

"I don't know." She did not know where the idea had come from. It was only that she didn't like not being able to account for herself.

Or maybe it was more than that. She didn't want to think about it.

74

He sat down on the edge of the bed. "Well, we know it's not just the Freaneys, but they were the first, for whatever that's worth."

"I wish you'd stop this, Brian."

"Why should I?"

"I told you, it's not right. Not for Patty. And what are you really going to do? You're a decent person."

"Do you think what happened to Patty was decent?"

She shook her head. She did not want him to turn into a savage, but maybe he already had.

"What do you want?" he asked.

"I want Patty."

"That's unrealistic. The only thing that's real for me is finding out who did it. And maybe that won't be enough. I don't know yet."

"It's been a week already."

"I know, but what can I do? I don't even know where to start, but I've started. I just haven't gotten anywhere. And I have to take time out to earn a living."

She ought to be doing that. She was a licensed practical nurse. She could have found a full-time job. But what if she were working in a hospital and started hearing the voice again? Or blacked out or walked in her sleep? She couldn't risk it.

Had she really driven the car in her sleep? She would have to begin checking the mileage.

They both stopped to listen at the sound of Patty's name. The radio was listing the previous victims. She started to tell him she didn't want to hear it. He raised his hand to silence her.

"So far, the poison has been found only in one-pound boxes of Red House sugar. However, health authorities have ordered all Red House sugar removed from stores in the area. The public is being warned not to use any Red House sugar in any size package, and to turn over all one-pound boxes of the brand to the nearest police station, hospital, or health clinic."

"Damn it," said Brian. "Why did Patty have to be the first?"

"I wish you wouldn't do that." It was so close. Patty might so easily have escaped taking the sugar and dying.

"Do what?" he asked.

"Those 'if onlys.' It's as if we could still change it. If we could do something a little bit differently."

He looked at her in surprise. "That's the way I feel. Only I don't get hopeful when I think about it."

After he left for work, she kept the radio on. She had to know more. It was a Valley Center station, and Brian listened to it in the morning for the weather, as well as the local news. That day the news was all about the cyanide poisonings, and warnings against Red House sugar.

That'll be the last of it, she thought. Unless they start on a different product.

Unless who did? She hated that faceless person.

She had her own faceless person, and she was afraid.

The next morning, predictably, Maynard Bundy's column in the *Journal* was devoted to the cyanide murders.

"It's a long arm," he wrote, "that reaches into happy homes, destroying and changing lives. The hand itself is invisible. The mind that controls it boasts a perverted kind of genius. It's a mind well versed in scientific know-how, with a brilliance worthy of the CIA for covering its trail."

"Bastard," said Brian, and read the paragraph aloud. "He's making the guy into a cult hero. Next they'll be selling T-shirts."

"You don't have to read it," Theresa told him.

He read on. He seemed to be hypnotized by Maynard Bundy.

"I'll kill him," he said.

"Who, Bundy?"

"Listen to this. 'A master plot of such clever conception deserves more than anonymity as its fate. This newspaper invites the White Powder Whiz Kid to turn himself in by calling the following private number and identifying himself to Yours Truly Maynard Bundy.'"

"Well," said Theresa, "that's one way of doing it."

"Listen, if the person wanted to advertise himself, he would have done it already. I don't think he wants to. This is just a publicity stunt for Bundy and it makes me want to strangle him."

Theresa began to cry. "It always happens. People like that always turn into heroes."

"No, they don't. It's just some problem with a creep like Bundy and his perverted fantasies. I think I'll tell him that. I'm going to call him from work."

"What will you tell him?"

"To get his head on before I lose it for him."

Brian called the number that was given in the paper.

"I am not the killer," he announced when Bundy was on the line. "I'm Brian Lonergan. My little girl was your buddy's first victim. Why don't you do a column on her instead of the worm who killed her? As a human being, she had a lot more to offer."

"I'd love to," Bundy purred. "When can you come in and tell me about her?"

This was unexpected. Brian had thought the man would be defensive. "What will you say about her?" he asked.

"Whatever you tell me. At the moment, all I know is her name and age and how she died."

"I don't know," Brian said. "I don't like the way you approach things."

"What do you mean?"

"It's lurid, the way you write about things. She was my kid. My only—" Something clicked in his mind. He remembered Cliff Baxter, Dorian's boy.

"She was our only child. And I don't like the way you played up this guy in your column. Made him out to be some kind of hero."

"Didn't you read the whole column?" Bundy asked. "I invited the man—or woman—to turn himself in. I had to sound positive about him so he'd want to get in touch with me. Don't you want to see him caught? Now when can you come in and tell me about your daughter?"

"I can't," said Brian. "I work. And I didn't mean it seriously about doing a column on her. I just get sick of people glorifying the murderers and forgetting the victims even had a face, not to mention a life and somebody who loved them."

"You have to go where the news is," Bundy said.

Brian hung up the phone.

He had called from his boss's office, but hadn't closed the door. He didn't realize anyone had heard him until Joe Williams, who had just finished ringing up a sale, turned and asked, "What was that all about?"

"Did you read Bundy's column in the paper this morning?"

"Nope."

"Then don't," said Brian. "It's a load of crap."

"I heard you talking about your little girl. Did they find anything yet?"

"Nothing."

Joe's customer, a wiry man with a stunning set of dentures, had stayed to listen. "You Lonergan?" he asked. "It's the damnedest thing, ain't it? You get a guy with a gun, at least he knows who he's shooting at. This guy don't even know who's going to get it, and he couldn't care less."

"That's right," said Joe. "You know what I've been thinking? Maybe they're all on the wrong track. Maybe it's a woman. When a man wants to kill somebody, he'll use his fists, or a gun, or even a two-by-four. Poison is a woman's way of knocking people off. Oh, shit, I'm sorry, Brian."

"Doesn't matter," said Brian. "It's bullshit anyway. And you're wrong about them being on the wrong track. They're not on any track."

"You know what's gonna happen," the customer told them. "All the other whackos are gonna get in on the act. They're gonna be putting it in salt, you name it."

"People don't eat as much salt as they do sugar," said Joe.

If only it had been salt. She never would have eaten salt. Brian realized he was doing the same thing he had told Theresa not to do. The "if onlys." You could make yourself crazy that way. But maybe it was inevitable. He tried to shut out the voices, the theories. Everybody had a piece of the action.

But it was theirs, too. It could happen to them. Although maybe not any longer, with all the publicity and the warnings.

It did happen again. No one understood how. It happened to Mitch Kennedy, a popular teacher and coach at Valley Center High School. It happened that same morning, but no one knew about it until afternoon, when another teacher went to investigate because Mitch hadn't reported for work that day.

"How can so many people eat the stuff?" Jess Morehouse asked in despair. "It's god-awful."

Investigator Lou Fiedler's eyebrows became crescents of surprise. "You tried it?"

"It's bitter. That's what they said. The doctors. Everybody. I don't have to try it."

"Too bad the guy was single," said Lou. "If he wasn't alone, maybe somebody could have found him in time."

"Maybe somebody would have had the radio on. He could have heard the warnings."

"That's some argument for getting married, huh? But they said he might have had a chance, if they got him in time."

"It's unbelievable. Just unbelievable," said Joe Williams, who kept a radio behind the counter.

Brian asked, "Did they say where it came from?"

"The sugar? From Saver Foods. Know where that is?"

"Is it a small place?"

"Yeah. Why?"

"Just asking. They all seem to be small places."

"I wonder why."

79

Brian thought he knew why. In a small store, especially an independent one, there was almost no chance of surveillance cameras.

He was doing it, finally. He was thinking like the killer. If he could just go on, follow the outward motions step by step, maybe they would lead him into the killer's mind. A reverse of the way the killer worked, but you had to start somewhere. He wondered when the boxes in Valley Center had been poisoned.

Theresa wondered, too. She hadn't listened to the radio. Brian told her about the death of the high school teacher when he came home.

"How do they know it was sugar?" she asked. "How can they tell it was sugar every time?"

"I guess that's not too hard if there's a box of sugar there and it's contaminated. Theresa, honey, let me ask you something."

The question alarmed her, and so did her reaction to it. She was suddenly unable to breathe.

"I want to know what you do all day," he said.

"Why?" It hadn't been as bad as she feared, but it was not completely off target.

"Now don't get me wrong. It's not that I think you should go back to work. It's just that I'm afraid of you being alone all the time, probably thinking about Patty."

She could not deny that she thought about Patty.

"I don't know what I do," she answered. And it was true.

"What do you mean?"

"I don't remember everything."

"That's not good, Theresa."

"Do you remember what you do all day? Could you account for every minute if somebody asked you?"

"You know that's not what I mean." He sounded injured.

She knew it wasn't. "Then what do you mean?" she asked.

"In general. I just want to know you're not—you know."

80

"Slowly going crazy?"

"I guess that's what I mean."

"I don't know that I'm not. But maybe I want to go crazy. It wouldn't hurt so much then."

That was what he had been afraid of. She could see it in his bleak, unsurprised look.

He didn't know how to tell her without seeming selfish. He needed her to be there. She understood that, too, And she needed not to be there. Or any place where the pain was.

She busied herself in the kitchen, hoping he wouldn't ask again. She found a package of ground beef in the refrigerator. She couldn't remember buying it. Probably he had picked it up on the way home. She began to shape it into hamburgers.

He pulled out a chair and sat down at the table. She wished he would go and watch television, or anything away from her.

"What did you mean when you said you don't remember everything?" he asked.

"I don't."

"But do you black out, or what?"

"I guess you could call it that." She put the frying pan on a burner to heat. He liked his hamburgers seared in a hot pan. He said it kept the juices in.

"Uh—" Another difficult question. "You haven't been drinking or anything, have you? Not that I'd blame you."

"No," she said. "Why do you ask? Don't you think I can have blackouts just because I lost my child?"

"I guess so." He hadn't wanted to ask. "But it's not good. I still think maybe you should see a doctor."

"Why? So they can make me not have blackouts? So I'll have more hours in the day when I can remember about Patty?"

"Listen, I lost Patty, too," he exploded.

"I was her mother."

"I don't think there's any way," he said, "of measuring who loves a child more, the mother or the father."

"That's not the point. I was more involved with her. She

81

was a bigger part of my life. My whole job was arranged so I could be home when Patty was home. The job was second. Patty was first."

"What about me?"

"But you can take care of yourself." She faltered. She knew it wasn't fair. He deserved her, too, but right now she couldn't handle it.

"When did they die?" she asked.

"Who?"

"Those people in Valley Center."

He had to think for a moment. "One of them was today, and the old couple—nobody knows exactly when. Last night, night before. Why?"

"I just wanted to know."

"Why, Theresa?"

His insistence frightened her. "Why not?" she snapped.

"It's all been in the newspaper."

"I didn't read the newspaper."

"Or listen to the radio? What do you do?"

They were back to that. "I watch game shows on television," she said.

"That could feel like a blackout."

He was trying to be funny. Did he think she could be jollied out of her grief? Nothing would ever be funny again.

After dinner, the headache came back. She needed to be alone, away from him, but he wouldn't understand. She put on her coat and went to get Alice's leash.

"Going out?" he asked. "Why didn't you tell me?"

"Just for a few minutes. I need some air."

"Wait, I'll go with you."

"Brian, I really want to be by myself."

"You've been alone all day."

"It's the dark. I want to take a walk in the dark."

"I thought you were afraid of the dark."

"Not outside."

82

He couldn't understand the difference. Outside, the darkness meant privacy. She couldn't have that in the daytime, not even in the woods, now that most of the leaves were gone. She opened the door and Alice charged down the steps, pulling at her leash.

Across the road, a shadow moved behind the dacron curtain in the Freaneys' living room. A bulky shadow. A square of light appeared and flickered. She moved into the darkness, away from the post lamp at the end of her driveway. Pressing a hand to her head, she tried to contain the throbbing. All around her, she felt the cool night. Cool, not cold as it had been when Patty died. The ache started to overcome her, but she slipped away from it.

Cheryl Freaney opened the door. Her look of expectant welcome dissolved into surprise. "Oh. Hi."

"Hi," said Michael.

"It's been a—" Cheryl cleared her throat. "It's been a long time. Come in." She glanced toward the living room. Always checking to be sure Leonard didn't mind.

"I'll only stay a minute," Michael said. "Just thought I'd drop by and say hello."

"Yeah. It's been—" Cheryl realized she had already said that.

"Not really so long," Michael reminded her. "It just seems that way."

"How about some coffee?"

"No, thanks. I can do without that."

"Oh, God," Cheryl gasped. "I can't tell you—"

"You don't have to. I just came over to say hello. How's Leonard?"

"He's watching television."

On the sound track, a car shrieked around a corner and stopped. Gunfire exploded.

Michael sat down at the kitchen table. He patted his pockets. They were empty. A pack of menthols lay on the table next to the sugar bowl. It was better than nothing. "May I?" he asked.

Cheryl blinked. "Go ahead. Help yourself."

Michael lit one and Cheryl handed him an ashtray. He began to wonder what he had come for. He seemed to have nothing to say. Maybe he just wanted to watch them in action.

Mark came into the kitchen. He stopped short when he saw Michael, mouthed "Hello," and opened the refrigerator.

"You just ate," Cheryl told him sharply. "Honestly, you'd think the kid would grow a little, he eats so much."

Mark gave her a withering glance. "All brains and no brawn," he muttered as he took out a stick of cheese and broke off a piece.

Only Michael noticed Leonard standing in the doorway. His show had given way to a commercial for laundry detergent.

"Brains, huh!" he scoffed. "Listen to who's got brains. You got brains where it counts, buddy?"

Mark's hand, still curled around the half-eaten piece of cheese, lowered itself from his mouth. Michael felt an irrational anger burst in his stomach like a mushroom cloud. This was none of his business, but he felt as though it was happening to him.

Leonard turned to their visitor. "Do you want to know how smart this kid is? He set the house on fire, that's what he did."

"When was that?" asked Michael.

"Couple of weeks ago."

"It was an accident." Mark's voice was hoarse.

"Yeah, because you're so dumb you don't even know what you're doing with that stuff," jeered his father. "You're one of those people who'll never amount to anything. You'll never be good for anything." To Michael, he said, "You want to know something? I don't think he's my kid. I think Cheryl must have been messing around."

"Screw you!" cried Cheryl. Mark fled down the hall to his room.

Leonard guffawed. "You got it wrong, baby. I said you didn't, is what I said."

"Have you been drinking?" Michael asked curiously. The laughter died away. Leonard regarded him with dull eyes.

"Or is this circus for my benefit?" Michael pursued.

"Your show's back on," Cheryl said quietly. Leonard raised his chin in defiance.

"I guess it's nothing unusual," said Michael. "And I realize I invited myself over, but that's not a nice thing to say about your wife, especially in front of other people. Or about your kid."

"Not my kid," Leonard maintained.

"If you feel that strongly, why don't you put him up for adoption?"

Leonard grinned. He had a brilliant, toothpaste-commercial smile. "You'd like that, wouldn't you? You want the little bastard, you take him." He went back to the living room and turned the television louder.

Cheryl's face was glazed and aloof. It was her way of withdrawing when the family tensions got too much for her.

"He doesn't mean it," she said. "He just gets mad sometimes."

"Quite a lot of times," Michael observed.

Cheryl bristled but said nothing. Michael crushed out his cigarette.

"I've got to go. Just wanted to see how everything was."

Cheryl said, "I'm glad you're feeling better."

Without thinking, Michael asked, "What do you mean?"

"Well, you know."

A mistake. He looked at her squarely. "No, I don't. I have no idea." He left, and heard the door close behind him.

He untied his dog from the lamppost and walked slowly along the road. He did not want to go home. Not for a damn long time. He enjoyed his freedom, being out on this moonlit night with just a faint bite in the air. It wasn't often that he got to do this.

Maybe he would never go back. It might be better all around if he didn't. He would go away somewhere and get a job. And live. He could do it. He was strong. He should have done it long ago. He had just been too responsible, but in retrospect, that was a shortsighted reason.

He walked to the end of the row and then back, trying to work out a plan. On the surface it didn't seem so difficult, but when he thought about the details, he could see that there were problems.

And then he was back at the Freaneys' house. He could hear their television through the closed windows.

Hatred welled in him at the sight of Leonard sitting in his easy chair, with a calcified brain that probably couldn't remember what he had done so many years ago. Twenty-one years ago. Or was it twenty-two? Mercifully, she couldn't remember, either. But it was still there. Still a part of her, and always would be.

And Leonard had never changed. Leonard saw nothing wrong with himself or with what he did, even his rages. He never saw himself as losing control. It was always somebody else's fault.

Twenty-one years ago.

We haven't finished, Leonard Freaney, Michael thought as he walked on. We haven't finished with you yet.

13

Maynard Bundy wrote again about the poisonings.

"When a function as basic to life as eating becomes fraught with the danger of sudden and terrible death," he told his readers, "then the very fabric of our being is destroyed. People are running scared these days. You can't blame them, when an innocent coffee break can mean the end of life. In the supermarkets, customers check the seals and inspect the packaging of everything they buy. Six deaths have brought about the total dislocation of our daily lives. Nothing will ever be the same again, for we will always remember. Such is the impact of one man or woman, the Cyanide Killer."

"Oh, shit!" exclaimed Brian.

Theresa closed her eyes. She was tired of everything. "I wish we could go away someplace where nobody knows us," she said.

"You know something? I'm willing to consider the possibility that Bundy's doing it all himself to get attention. Oh, God, listen to this." Brian read aloud, "'According to its very nature, poison doesn't do anything until it is taken. However unintentionally, by eating that sugar, the victims brought about their own deaths.' The guy's sick, you know that? He's sick." While finishing his coffee, Brian composed a letter to the editor of the *Journal,* denouncing Maynard Bundy as a sick screwball. He mailed it on the way to work.

Later that day, the killer read Bundy's column and then sat on his bed in a semitrance, not really thinking about it.

In spite of what might have sounded like praise, he felt no elation. By his hand, theoretically, people had died. He looked down at his hand, at the newspaper still on his lap, and he couldn't feel that that hand had killed anybody. It was too remote and impersonal. He felt no rage. Only the desire to eradicate, and it hadn't worked. That alone made him angry, but not very angry. He couldn't get excited. Nothing stirred him any more. He wondered if he was afraid. He should have been afraid, but there didn't seem any reason to be. The police were nowhere near him. They couldn't trace him. The only person who had even come close was Brian Lonergan, but he hadn't known how close he was.

It had been a good plan. An excellent one. He was proud of himself. The only thing wrong was that it hadn't worked, and now the heat was on. If he tried it again, he might be pushing his luck. It was really too bad.

Theresa opened her refrigerator and was shocked to see how empty it was. Brian would be coming home soon. She hadn't even thought about dinner until now.

She put on her shoes and reached for a sweater. Her mind spun. Was it summer? Winter? Fall?

It was November. She took a heavy jacket.

Cheryl Freaney, raking the leaves from her lawn, greeted her cheerfully. "Gorgeous day. I just wanted to be out, so I decided to rake."

"Yes," said Theresa, and looked in her purse to be sure she had enough money. It was too late for the bank—she thought. She had forgotten to wear her watch.

Cheryl wandered across the road. "Did you quit your job? I never see you going to work any more."

"Yes, I did." Theresa opened the car door. If she were to back out right now, she would run over Cheryl.

"I have to get going," she explained. "I forgot to buy dinner."

"Why don't you ask Brian to pick up something?"

"I don't want to bother him." She didn't want him to know she had forgotten.

"I just thought it seemed silly for you to make the trip." Cheryl stepped out of the way.

"It's very silly." Theresa got into her car. Cheryl stood by the ditch, looking snubbed. Too bad, Theresa told herself, but through long habit, she was afraid to leave anyone angry with her. She began to chatter. "I just don't know where the day went. I really don't. It's suddenly four o'clock and I don't even remember what I was doing all day."

"If there's any way I can help . . ."

"It's okay." Theresa turned on the engine and backed out of her driveway. In the rearview mirror she could see Cheryl watching her. The whole day. She couldn't explain it. Maybe she ought to find another job and get back her sense of purpose. But even that seemed pointless. Everything did, and there was no way that she could think of to change it.

She drove to the Pine Glen Market, hoping Dorian Baxter wouldn't be there. But Dorian was. Theresa picked up a basket and hurried down the aisle. She stood for a while gazing at the packaged meats before she could remember why she was there. And then she couldn't decide. They had less money now, without her income. They could really only afford hamburgers, but she wanted to give him something nice. She was acutely aware of Dorian, and that Brian had once been involved with her. And that she, Theresa, was fast fading out of the picture. Just dissolving bit by bit and not being able to stop herself. And someday she would be all gone, except maybe physically, and what would they do with her shell? She supposed at that point it wouldn't matter.

She selected a ham steak, never minding the price, and a

90

package of frozen peas and onions. When she reached the counter, Dorian tilted her head and looked at her with tragic eyes.

"Theresa, what can I say? It must be the most terrible thing that can happen to a person."

"Yes, it is," said Theresa.

"Brian was in here the other day."

"I know. He told me."

"He was asking questions. I told him the police already asked me."

"Dorian, if you don't mind, I'd rather not talk about it."

"Of course, dear. I'm sorry." Dorian turned her attention to the groceries.

I wish we could go away someplace where nobody knows us.

"Are you still working?" Dorian asked.

"No, I'm not. I just forgot about dinner."

Dorian looked at her. Forgot? To feed Brian? "You're not going back to work?"

"No," said Theresa.

"Wouldn't it help if you had something to do?"

"It might."

"I know it's none of my business."

No. It isn't. Theresa slipped the change into her purse.

"Give my love to Brian."

She remembered Dorian's parting words, but did not remember leaving the store or getting into her car. Suddenly she was driving up the road toward home.

I'm crazy, she thought. I've gone completely crazy.

Shaking from the experience, she turned into the trailer park. The post lamps were beginning to come on. It was almost dark, and the sun had been out when she went to the store. Had it? Yes, she remembered Cheryl raking leaves in the afternoon sunshine.

A good hour, at least. Where had she been? And driving her car, too.

91

She would not tell anyone. Not even Brian. There was no one she could trust. It was a good thing she had reached home before he did. She pulled into their driveway and parked.

A voice behind her said, "Hey, that was some trip to the store. What did you do, get lost?"

Cheryl stood at the rail of her sun deck. Theresa simply looked at her, not knowing what to answer.

"You haven't seen my son, have you?" Cheryl asked. "He's just disappeared, and if Leonard comes home—"

"Thank God," said Theresa, "that Leonard isn't my problem."

She went into the house and took her groceries out of the bag. Her heart was pounding. She did not know why. Maybe because of the threat of Leonard. It stirred some vague fear in her left over from her childhood. She could only hope that Mark would grow up fast and be able to cope with his father.

But it was never fast enough.

Brian did not ask what she had done that day. But when she went to bed, she dreaded the morning. What new craziness would it bring? And how long could she last without anyone finding out?

She did not get up when Brian did. She did not want to be asked questions, or to hear about Maynard Bundy.

Then she remembered Dorian. She saw herself, by contrast, as a sodden wretch, and she got out of bed and combed her hair to join him at the breakfast table.

"Do you think I should get a job?" she asked.

If she had a job, maybe the crazy spells would go away. Or maybe she would simply mess up her work.

He looked up from the newspaper. "I think you should do whatever feels right," he said. "But you might be more comfortable if you kept busy."

"I feel guilty sitting around all day while you work."

He reached out and put his hand over hers. "Don't worry

about that. I'd go to work even if we didn't need the money. It takes my mind off things."

"Don't you ever feel as if you might break down in front of people?"

He thought it over. "Not really. Not while I'm talking to a customer. If I ever felt near the breaking point, I think I'd go out and sit in my car for a while."

He leaned toward her and pushed the hair back from her forehead. "Are you really all right, Theresa? What do you do all day by yourself? Do you just think about Patty?"

She answered carefully. "Sometimes I sleep." It was bad, but not as damning as the blackouts. "I'd probably think about Patty no matter what I was doing."

He closed the newspaper and got up from the table. "Maybe a hospital job would keep you busy. You could take a full-time job now, but don't think I'm pressing you. I just thought maybe a big change like that would help."

"Maybe." She knew better than to argue. But she couldn't be responsible for patients when she wasn't even able to account for herself.

Later in the morning there was a knock at the door. Alice jumped up from her nap and began to bark. Theresa tried to ignore the knock, but it came again. Someone, whoever it was, knew she was home. Pushing Alice out of the way, she answered the door and found a strange young woman in a gray pantsuit standing on the steps.

"Hello, I'm Larry Haynes from the *Journal*."

It couldn't have been "Larry," Theresa thought. It must have been "Mary."

"You're Mrs. Lonergan, right?" said the woman. "I think it must have been your husband who wrote a letter to the paper about one of Mr. Bundy's columns."

"My husband's not here," said Theresa.

"That's okay, I don't want to bother him at work, but I'd

93

just like to talk to you and get your side of the story. Your husband seemed to think Mr. Bundy wasn't showing enough sympathy for the victims and their families."

"I'd rather not talk about it." Theresa started to close the door. "It's all right if you want to see my husband at work. He's at Reynolds Home Center in the village."

Instead of retreating, the woman pushed forward, planting her foot on the threshold. "I'd like to talk to you, as the little girl's mother. I think we might get a more sensitive story."

"I'm not interested in your stories," Theresa replied, "and I don't want to talk to you."

"Just a few questions. It won't take but a minute." And Larry/Mary Haynes was in her living room, looking around. "This is a cute place you have here. It's really nice. How long have you lived in this park?"

"Three years." Theresa had given up and lost all feeling.

"It's really cute. Could I see the rest of it?"

"Help yourself."

Ms. Haynes missed the sarcasm. With Alice following her and growling suspiciously, she walked to the end of the hall, peered into the master bedroom, and started back. At the closed door midway down the hall, she stopped.

"Is this your little girl's room? Could I see it?"

"Go ahead." If you must. Theresa turned away. For a moment there was nothing but silence, and then she heard the door close again.

"I know it's terrible of me to intrude," said Ms. Haynes, "but I think it's a story that needs to be told."

Theresa said, "I've often wondered whether reporters even knew when they were intruding and that it was terrible, or do they just go ahead anyway?"

"Like everybody else, we have our jobs to do."

Theresa was about to respond when Ms. Haynes continued, "Could we sit down and talk for a minute? Just a minute."

Why am I letting her do this to me? Theresa perched on an arm of the sofa.

"Can you tell me something about that night? It happened in a neighbor's house, didn't it?"

Theresa gave an inaudible sigh. It was better that the story should come from her than from Cheryl Freaney. She told the reporter all she could remember of the events that led to Patty's death. Of seeing her there on the Freaneys' bathroom floor, and the ride to the hospital.

"And she was your only child?" Ms. Haynes asked softly. "Do you think you might want to have another one now?"

Theresa shook her head, clenching her teeth to stifle a sob. "I can't," she managed to say after the sob had passed. "I can't have any more children."

"Is it a medical problem?"

"Obviously. Is there any other reason why a person couldn't have children? I think I've taken enough of your time." She could not remember whose time had been taken, or why. Something was pressing on her head. The migraine would start at any moment. She saw Ms. Haynes to the door and locked it after her.

The next thing she knew it was afternoon, and she was opening the door of her car outside a Purwin Farm and Feed Store.

14

She got into her car and quickly closed the door. Then she looked around to see whether anyone had noticed her.

A grizzled man in a red jacket crossed the parking area and climbed into the cab of a pickup truck. A woman with a small child in tow browsed among a selection of flowerpots under a green fiberglass canopy.

No one seemed to be aware of her. Apparently she had done nothing odd. She had been driving her car like a normal person and had probably been inside the store. Yet she hadn't bought anything. Her hands were empty. She looked for her purse. It was not in the car. She felt in her pockets and found her wallet and driver's license.

How could they not have noticed her? What had she been doing?

She sat in her car and studied the outside of the store, the lay of the land, trying to figure out where she was. Nearly every large community had a Purwin store.

The familiar dread and fear washed over her. She felt so helpless, suddenly and unaccountably finding herself in a strange place. It hadn't happened very often since her marriage. Only now, after Patty's death. It was as though her life were a patchwork quilt and half the patches were missing.

But this time she had been driving. It was like the other

day after she left the Pine Glen Market. How could she have driven the car and not had an accident?

The coldness inside the car began to seep through to her. She saw that she was wearing one of Brian's jackets, actually a checkered plaid shirt with a quilted lining. It was not warm enough. She started the engine and turned on the heater. Instantly the car began to warm up. That meant the engine was warm. She hadn't been here very long.

She had never seen this store before, but she could hardly walk up to someone and ask where she was. She drove out of the parking lot and onto the road that ran past the store, taking a guess as to her direction. Eventually she would come to a sign.

She drove through an unfamiliar village and out onto a highway. She drove past fields, farms, and rolling hills. She had gone several miles before she found the sign she had been looking for. PORT JERVIS, 8 MI., it said, and pointed to the left.

Port Jervis was twenty miles from Pine Glen. She had no idea in which direction she was traveling. The sun was vaguely overhead. For all she knew, she might even have been in Pennsylvania. Or New Jersey. She looked at the passing license plates. Three in a row were from New York State. At least she was on home territory, more or less. She drove until she saw a sign that said JCT. 209. Thank God. When she reached the junction she turned in the opposite direction from Port Jervis, and half an hour later she was home.

She did not remember the visit from Mary/Larry Haynes until the next morning, when Brian showed her the article. The name was Bari Haines.

"Why didn't you tell me?" he asked in wounded tones.

Without thinking, she replied, "I forgot."

"You what?"

"It was because of the letter you wrote about Bundy. She came over. I told her to go and see you, but she wouldn't. And then something happened and I forgot about her."

97

"What do you mean? What happened?"

"Just—something."

"I think you'd better tell me."

She felt herself crumbling into despair. And then she realized that she didn't have to tell him. No one could force her. She was an adult now and could do what she thought best.

"Honey?" he said, prompting her.

"No, thank you, Brian. I'm not going to talk about it."

"But if it was bad enough to make you forget this—"

"It's my own problem and I'm going to work it out for myself."

"But that's why we have each other."

She had not thought of it that way. She had never been accustomed to "having" people when she needed them. They had always failed her or betrayed her.

"I'm sorry," she said. "I can't talk about it right now."

He had to be satisfied with that. "Okay. Just remember I'm here." He returned to the article. "You showed her Patty's room?"

"She opened the door and looked. I didn't go with her."

"I wish she could have come when we were both here."

"So do I."

"And she even found out we can't have more kids. Why'd you tell her that?"

"She asked, damn her. You know, it takes a lot of energy to argue with people."

"Maybe we should have Alice trained as an attack dog, to attack reporters."

"Attack everybody, except United Parcel and people like that. And relatives," she added, seeing the way he looked at her.

"And neighbors?"

"No more exceptions."

"It seems hard to believe," he said, "but someday this thing is going to go away."

"Not all of it."

"No, not the worst part, but I mean the attention. When the killer gets nailed there will be one big, final thing—they'll probably want to know how we feel about that, and then it will be over."

"Then they'll have a trial," she said. "It won't be over."

"Until the trial, and then afterward. Once they wrap it up, it's finished."

She rested her head in her hand. "They'll never wrap it up."

"Somebody will, one way or another. If I have to spend the rest of my life, I'm not letting that creep get away with it."

She did not respond. So far the creep had gotten away with six murders, and neither the police nor Brian had accomplished anything.

"I know what you're thinking," he said. "If we all felt the same way—the other families—"

"Brian, what can you do?"

"I've got some hunches. I can ask questions."

"Everywhere you've been so far, the police were there first."

"I've been working on it. I'm trying to think like the killer. Why would a person do a thing like that? What sort of person is it? That's one approach. And then you have to take into consideration where you can get cyanide. Who would have access to it?"

"And?"

"Chemical plants. Industry. Places like that. And pesticides. This is farming country. It's probably everywhere they sell farm supplies."

She sat looking at her hands, not wanting him to see her face. He must never know about her unexplained visit to the Purwin store. He was still talking, but she couldn't hear him. She only knew that she wanted him out of there. He must get out. Now. She had to check the trunk of her car.

Finally he closed the newspaper, pushed it toward her, and

got up from the table. She tried to slow the thing that was racing inside her while he put on his coat and kissed her goodbye. She watched from the kitchen window as he backed out of the driveway. She watched until he had turned the corner, and then she went outside, still in her bathrobe and slippers, and looked in the glove compartment first. Nothing but maps, a flashlight, the insurance card.

Next she opened the trunk. She checked everything. The jack. The tool box. The half gallon of radiator coolant. Two dirty rags, a piece of chamois, a coffee can full of sand for winter traction. A wad of fresh green paper down in a well beside the spare tire. She pulled it out.

An empty paper bag. She could not remember anything about it, where it had come from, what it had held. It hadn't been in the car two weeks ago when she took out the Phillips screwdriver to tighten the side-view mirror. She tried to think, tried to remember, but her brain felt like a swamp. She thought of going to all the Purwin stores to see what color their bags were, but someone might remember her from an earlier visit. A visit of which she had no memory. She took the bag into the house and threw it away.

That night Brian telephoned Harry Grover and Jennie Cardo Baldwin, the two people he knew personally who had lost someone to the cyanide killer. Jennie Baldwin's husband was on a night shift and she had to stay home with the children. Harry Grover, who lived only a few doors away from the Lonergans, came over.

Harry had started a beard and lost weight since Marylou's death. He looked far older than his thirty years.

They talked about the murders for a while, and then Brian explained what he was doing to try to find the killer.

"What for?" asked Harry. "Aren't the police working on it?"

"The more heads, the better," Brian replied. "Somebody might come up with something. Do you realize that even now the police have absolutely nothing to go on?"

100

"Nothing? No leads?"

"Nothing at all. And I don't think the killings are going to go on, either. The guy's had his fun. Now the trail is just going to get cold."

Theresa did not join them, but stayed in the kitchen, listening. "Would you like some coffee?" she asked Harry.

He looked at her for a moment while his lips tightened to a grim line. He said, "I don't drink it any more."

"I don't blame you," she replied.

Brian offered a beer and Harry accepted. When Brian had talked further about his investigation and invited Harry to join it, Harry's head dropped forward. He seemed as tired as Theresa felt.

"I don't know," he said. "I've got two kids to look after. I don't get to spend much time with them as it is."

"Who's been taking care of them while you work?" Theresa asked.

"My mother's there now, but she can't stay much longer. She has to get home to my dad. I might even have to send the kids back with her." He looked desolate as he said it. She thought again of the green paper bag. There was so much that was unexplained. She was afraid of what it might all mean.

"It was just a thought," said Brian. "Probably childish. It's just that—"

"Yeah, I know. You have to do something. I envy you that," Harry said.

"You have your kids," Brian pointed out.

"You have your wife."

They were silent for a while. Theresa thought: He can always get another wife, but you can't replace your own child. She wondered how she would feel if Brian were to die.

Harry said, "You know, you could sue for this. You can sue for mental anguish, and who knows? In your case, maybe for loss of support in your old age."

"Sue?" said Brian. "Just—sue? You have to have a defendant, but who's responsible? They don't even know that."

"Sue the Red House company. You ought to be able to get something out of them."

Theresa turned toward the sink so they wouldn't see her tears.

"That's probably what I'm going to do," Harry was saying. "This guy I know who's a lawyer said there's precedents for bringing suit on the ground the package is too easy to tamper with."

"Hell, who would ever think of anybody poisoning a box of sugar in a store?" said Brian. "You can't put everything in tamper-proof packages. The whole thing is so—I mean, who'd expect it?"

"What else can we do? It's the only thing we have. With her gone, you know, my whole life is wrecked. The kids', too."

After Harry left, Brian took another beer from the refrigerator. "Can't blame the guy. He wants to get back somehow, just like I do, but the Red House company isn't at fault. I want to get the real killer. I just want that pervert. I want to get my hands on him."

"Brian, please."

"Everybody thinks I'm crazy, that I'm chasing my own tail, but damn it, the police have nothing. So maybe I'm crazy. Okay."

"I'd rather you sue the company, Brian."

"Why?"

"I don't know. I'm afraid—" She couldn't tell him what she really feared. She was not even sure herself. "I just don't want you to be violent."

"Well, I am violent. And if that's the way I feel, then it's better I take it out where it belongs."

He stopped and listened. It had sounded like a knock on the door. Theresa instinctively tensed. She did not want to see anyone.

Before she could stop him, Brian went to answer it. She heard voices and Mark Freaney came in, shivering in a lightweight jacket. It was not even a jacket, really, but a navy blue work shirt with Scalzo Motors emblazoned on the back.

"They locked me out," Mark explained.

"Your father?" asked Brian.

Mark shrugged. "Who else? He told me to go put my bicycle in the shed. When I came back, the door was locked. The back door, too."

"Did your mother know you were out?"

"I guess so. She heard him tell me. Can I use your phone? I want to call John Reiss and ask if I can spend the night."

"Spend the night!" Brian exclaimed.

"Yeah. When he locks me out, he means it. I want to check on the Reisses before I go all the way over there. It's pretty cold out. So if I could use your phone . . ."

"Wait a minute." Brian picked up the telephone. "Your parents must be nuts. What's your number?"

Mark told him the number and Brian dialed. Mark said, "You're just going to get me in worse trouble."

"Why did they lock you out for doing what you were told to do?" Theresa asked.

"'Cause I forgot to put my bicycle away."

"Yes, but—"

"Cheryl?" said Brian into the phone. "Did you know your son is locked out of the house?"

Her voice came faintly over the wire, high-pitched and whining. "I know, but I can't do anything about it. You know how he is."

"I know how you both are. He's a bastard and you let him get away with it. You don't even try to protect your own kids. That's what parents are supposed to do. Protect their kids. I know quite a lot about child abuse from what Theresa went through when she was little. There are laws against this sort of thing, Cheryl. Now, are you going to let him in?"

"I can't."

"It's cold out there. Do you want me to call the police?"

Mark interrupted. "I don't want to go home, Mr. Lonergan. I'd rather just go to John Reiss's."

Theresa wanted to put her arm around him, but held back. Physical demonstration was still alien to her. Brian relayed

103

the boy's message to Cheryl, listened for another moment, then handed the phone to Mark, who dialed his friend.

"What did she say?" Theresa asked.

Brian replied, "Said she couldn't let him in. She has to obey the master."

"I've seen her with bruises, too."

"I know. But do you know what she said when I threatened her with the police? 'He's not a bad man, Brian. He doesn't mean to be cruel. He's just strict and he loses his temper sometimes.' Can you beat that?"

Theresa felt a sickness in her stomach. A terrible dread. Because of what Leonard reminded her of? Or something about Leonard himself? She couldn't tell.

Mark hung up the phone. "I'm going over to the Reisses'," he said.

"Good, I'm glad you have a place," Theresa told him. "You know you can stay here any time. Remember that."

"Thanks for everything."

"Wait. Take a coat, at least," said Brian.

"That's okay. I'm warm now, and I'll run all the way. I just wanted to find out first."

He was gone. Theresa said, "I hate that man."

"I'll bet you do. It brings it all back, doesn't it?" Brian replied.

"I don't know if that's why. Maybe it is. But I hate him for himself, too."

"He's not exactly lovable."

"I can understand her, though. With people like that, you get so afraid. And you need them. You have to believe they're not really bad."

"You were a child, Theresa. She's a grown woman."

"Cheryl doesn't seem like the sort of person who couldn't cope, but she probably is, or she never would have gotten into that relationship in the first place."

"Still, it's worse for the kids. They had no choice. And you . . ." He pulled her close to him.

104

She felt tears burn in her eyes and fall onto his shoulder. "At least, whatever she had—Patty—at least she had a good life."

"Yes," he said, stroking her back, "we gave her that. We gave her a good life. Such as it was."

15

"I have something to tell you," Dorian said after Cliff had left the room.

Brian waited, but did not look at her. He suddenly wasn't sure he wanted to know about it.

She asked, "Don't you think he's a terrific kid?"

"All kids are terrific," Brian replied.

"I don't mean it that way. I'm not bragging. It's just that I wanted you to know, because of what happened—I wanted you to know—" She stopped and tried to rethink what she was saying. "Remember just before I went to the city that time?"

"Sure, I remember."

"Well, I told everybody I was married in the city, but I wasn't. I didn't even have a boyfriend. Cliffie—I don't know how to tell you this, Brian."

"Maybe I already have an idea of what you're trying to tell me," he said.

"Huh?"

"Maybe I got the idea from a friend of yours. Henry Aiken."

"Hank? What the hell does he know?"

"It's possible that he's not as dumb as he looks."

"Then if you already knew about it—"

"I didn't know. Hank didn't mean to spill it, and when he did, I wasn't really sure he knew anything. He could have been just jealous."

106

"You think that's what happened, don't you? You don't believe it's true."

"If you say it's true, then I believe it. And I understand your timing, but—"

"You were already married when I came home with him." She regarded him steadily with her clear, untrustworthy eyes. He realized that that was why he disliked those eyes in spite of their beauty.

"Thanks," he said, and meant it. She could have disrupted his new marriage, but she hadn't. If she had let him know in time, he would have married her and he probably would have regretted it.

"I know why you told me just now. You wanted to let me know I still have a kid, and I appreciate it." He wondered whether she had really meant it that way, or whether she had something up her sleeve. "Only thing is, it's not just a matter of having a kid. They're not interchangeable."

"I understand what you're saying. Nothing can replace the kid you lost. I just thought you might want to know. It was in the newspaper that your wife can't have any more."

"Yes, I know it was, thanks to an aggressive bitch of a reporter."

"Is it true?"

"Of course it's true." Did she think it had been a play for sympathy?

"Freshen your drink?" she asked. His glass was only half empty. She had called him at work and asked him to stop by on his way home, just for a drink. She had made it sound so casual, and then she had dropped the bombshell. It hadn't turned out to be quite the blockbuster she probably expected.

He had phoned Theresa to say he would be delayed. He hadn't told her how or where. He felt furtive and treacherous, but her flat, listless monotone made him think she probably didn't care.

"How's Theresa?" Dorian asked as she added ice and whiskey to his glass. "Is she any better?"

"Better than what?"

"Any better than she was. You said she was a wreck after losing your daughter."

"Yes, she took it pretty hard. Still does. Why, is there something wrong with that?"

"I saw her the other day in the store. She seemed kind of confused."

"It's been very hard on her, naturally."

"Doesn't make it any easier for you, though, does it? After all, it was your loss, too."

"Yes, but you have to understand Theresa. She's had a rough life." He felt defensive. But what Dorian said was true. Theresa seemed to forget that Brian was suffering, too. As if Patty had been especially hers.

"A lot of times," Dorian said, "people even break up over things like that. And you know something? It can turn out to be a good thing. You can start your life all over again, like you were a different person."

"Maybe," he said noncommittally.

"Did you ever think maybe she really doesn't care about you any more? Could be, she's just too far gone."

"For God's sake, it only just happened. We're both still bleeding."

"Oh, I understand that. Maybe it will all work out. But if it doesn't, Brian, I just want you to know I'm here."

"Yeah," he said, staring into his drink.

"I care what happens to you. I want you to know that. I want you to have a life, and not be dragged down when there's nothing you can do for her anyway."

He didn't like this. He had been prepared for it, but he found it more disturbing than he had expected. Maybe because Dorian tempted him. It wasn't love, but she was alive. She was offering herself. He could have her any way he wanted, and maybe Theresa wouldn't even care.

"I'd better get on home." He set down his empty glass.

"Do you think she'll notice?" Dorian asked.

"She might. Look, did you happen to remember anything more?"

"About what?"

"About who might have been messing around in the store. Do you recognize most of the people who go in there?"

She looked wounded. She had expected him to show more interest in his relationship with Cliffie. It didn't occur to her that he might have trouble absorbing it.

"Most, but not all," she said. "I told you, I don't see what goes on. It wouldn't have entered my mind to watch for somebody exchanging boxes of sugar."

"You don't remember the different people who bought sugar. Do a lot of people buy one-pound boxes of sugar?"

"Enough. I don't keep track."

"Thanks, Dorian."

"Come again, will you? It's good for Cliffie to have a man around."

"He doesn't know, I hope."

"Do you think I'm crazy? But if you ever decide to take me up on my offer, I'll tell him then. And we can be a family. Think about it, Brian. You could have a kid again. Your own kid. And with me, you could have more."

"I'll see you, Dorian."

He hurried down a flight of stone steps to his car. There was a bad taste in his mouth, and it wasn't the whiskey. He wondered if it might have been the attraction he felt in spite of himself, and the guilt because of it. Ever since Patty's death, Theresa had been rejecting him. He needed the closeness, and she pushed him farther away. Dorian was ready to give him what he needed, but he couldn't kick Theresa when she was down.

He hated the whole mess. He wanted it to be finished, but that wouldn't happen until they found the killer.

***

109

He took the next day off from work. They were lenient with him. He had had a week when Patty died, and now they gave him this. They did not ask why he wanted it.

He was looking for a person. It had to be a person who knew about poisons. Who would think in terms of poison. The craziness, he supposed, would have come later.

He drove to Valley Center, then through it to its western edge, where the high school stood on a broad, low hill. Years ago, it had been his school. And Dorian's and Henry Aiken's. Thirteen years ago they had been graduated. If he had known what was ahead, would he have wanted to leave the place?

He parked in the students' lot and went inside. He didn't need to orient himself. Up a flight of stairs and down the hall on the left. The door to the chemistry lab was closed. Through its glass pane he could see a class in progress. The teacher, new since his time, was a bearded young man who sat perched on the edge of his desk, gesturing animatedly, obviously enjoying his own lecture.

Brian had timed his arrival. In another minute the bell rang, doors opened, and students erupted into the hall. He had to wait while two leggy blondes made a play for the teacher, and then he plunged in.

"Hello, I'm Brian Lonergan. I used to go to school here. Have you been teaching here long?"

"Three years. Frank Price." They shook hands.

"I'll make it fast," said Brian, "before the next round. It's about the cyanide poisonings."

"Village police? State police?"

"No police."

"Oh, hell, I know who you are. It was your little girl, right?"

"Right. And I don't feel anything's happening."

"Well, they sure asked a lot of questions."

"Do you mind a few more? They'll probably be the same ones. I'm trying to figure out where a person would get cyanide."

110

"Not here," said Frank Price. "I can assure you, we don't keep poisonous materials in our lab, not for high school kids."

"Okay, next question. You've been here three years. Did you ever have any students who were bright but sort of flaky? Strange?"

"They asked me that, too. I can't remember all of them, of course, but none that stand out like that. I'm afraid it would be kind of confidential anyway. I'd really like to help you, Mr.—"

"Brian. So even if you weren't being confidential, you don't think there's anything here. Anything I could get from you."

"Nothing. Negative. I told that to the police. But I'm with you, Brian. I understand what you're going through."

Everybody understood.

"You're definite about that?"

"Definite. And it's been on my mind a lot. I've been working on a—" He went around to the front of his desk, opened a drawer, and took out a white cardboard box. When he removed the cover, Brian saw glass bottles and strips of colored paper.

"People have gotten so scared," Price explained, "that I worked up this little kit. Maybe I'll try to market it, I don't know. It's a poison detection kit. These are all chemicals that will react in the presence of various poisons. Some change color, others give off an odor."

"What's the paper for?"

"That's litmus paper. Did you ever take chemistry?"

"No."

"Well, cyanides are alkaline, see. The paper doesn't tell much, but if the pink paper turns blue, at least you know you've got an alkali."

"Right," said Brian. He hadn't the haziest idea what it was all about. And the people who died had been taken by surprise. They would never have thought to test their sugar with litmus paper.

"Smart," he said as Frank put the box back in his drawer

and locked it. He hadn't noticed before that the drawer was kept locked.

"Well, I don't know," Frank said modestly. "I guess we all have to feel we're doing something."

"We certainly do." Behind him, the next class had been pouring in, rustling and talking. "Look, Frank, I just thought of something. If you invented that kit to test for cyanide—"

"And other poisons."

"Yeah, okay. Well, you must have had those poisons on hand to test it with, right? Where did you get stuff like that? I need to know."

Frank's face became set. He was going to be stubborn, Brian thought. Then Frank grinned.

"I don't think anybody else could get them there," he said. "They knew I was a chemistry teacher. I know a guy who works there. It's an industrial plant. They let me buy a small quantity off them, but I don't think they'd sell it to just anybody."

"What plant? Where is it?"

"It's not around here. About twenty-five, thirty miles away. It's not likely the killer would have gotten it there, but the police asked me not to give out information, just in case some other nut got cute ideas."

"I'm not another nut," said Brian.

"I know you're not. But it's not around here, and the killings are all local, so I don't think that's your answer."

This, obviously, was as far as Frank intended to go. Brian thanked him and left. He felt frustrated. His hands had reached out and grasped air. Still, the teacher was probably right. This was obviously a local crime. If the killer had had knowledge of, or access to, an industrial plant some thirty miles away, the poisonings undoubtedly would have taken a different geographical spread.

Yet he couldn't help feeling that there must have been more than this. Somebody—the killer—knew all the facts. And unless he was a hermit, those who were close to him must have been able to guess something. It was probably a case of not knowing what they knew. Or denying it.

He visited two community colleges and the State University at New Paltz, with no better results. He visited drugstores in Valley Center and Pine Glen, and drew a blank there, too. They did not carry cyanide per se. "What for?" they asked. And everywhere he went, the police had been there first. It was discouraging, he thought, that the police had no better ideas than he had himself.

The day was nearing its end. A whole day with nothing to show for it, except that he had used up a lot of gas and maybe eliminated some possibilities. He had learned that cyanide was not obtainable in high schools, and only under controlled conditions in most colleges. He learned that you didn't just walk into a drugstore and buy it.

He knew it was used as an insecticide, which left him with the obvious source for that—farm supply centers. There were Purwin Farm and Feed Stores widely scattered throughout the area. He didn't know where they all were, but he knew there was one five miles north of Valley Center, and he drove there.

"Not much call for insecticides this time of year," said the man behind the cashier's desk.

"It could have been bought earlier," Brian suggested. "In the summer or fall, maybe."

"Listen, fella, I already told you guys everything I know, which is nothing."

"I'm not from the police."

"What are you, a reporter?"

"Hardly. I have a personal interest."

Brian explained what his personal interest was. The man became grudgingly contrite. Probably embarrassed. It had not, after all, happened to him. That tended to make people feel vaguely guilty, Brian had noticed.

"Well, what can I do for you?" the man asked.

"Do you carry anything with cyanide in it?"

113

"Why?"

"I want to know where it came from."

"Why, you think it came from here?"

"Now look, let's start this again," Brian said. "I'm asking you because I know it's not that easy to get hold of cyanide. I do know that farmers sometimes use it to kill bugs. So I asked myself, where do the farmers get it? I thought of farm supply stores. This is the one closest to where I live. It's nothing against you personally or your store. It's only a question."

"The police already asked me all them questions."

"Even if I were to ask the police what you told them, they wouldn't tell me," Brian explained patiently.

"That's between you and the police," said the man. "They already asked all them questions."

"Do you mind if I look around?"

"Be my guest."

Brian wandered among the shelves of sprays and insecticides, studying their ingredients. He found such names as malathion and diethyl phosphorothioate, but no cyanide. It might have been in a different form. He knew that much about chemistry, but very little more. It was no wonder they kept telling him to leave it up to the police. He had no background, as well as no official status that would open doors.

Wait a minute. He stopped at the end of the aisle. That had been pure cyanide. Hadn't it? Or at least a pure white powder that mixed invisibly with sugar. And powerful enough so that, even mixed with the sugar, it could kill almost instantly.

He went back to the cash register. The man was busy with a customer. When the customer left, the man tried to ignore Brian.

"Is cyanide readily available?" Brian asked.

"Depends," said the man. "Readily available to who?"

"Anybody who wants it."

"I wouldn't say so. It's readily available to people who've got use for it."

"Pure cyanide?"

"Like I said, there's certain things they use it for. I guess they can get it for that if they want it. Look, I only work here. Why don't you go ask a chemist or something?"

"Thanks. You've been very helpful." Brian left the store and went out to his car. He wondered if there was any sense in going on with this. But his daughter had been murdered. He couldn't just leave it at that. It was as though the killer was mocking him, and Patty, too, if he didn't try to do something.

Maybe he could get some information from the police. They wouldn't tell him much, but anything would help. He started down the highway and soon was driving through Valley Center. The lights were coming on and the neon signs were shining in the early November dusk. Just ahead of him was the Scalzo Motors showroom, bright with posters, bunting, and gleaming new automobiles. He could see Leonard Freaney at his desk beside the window. He saw Leonard turn to look out at the street, and saw the sudden stiffening as Leonard recognized his car.

The traffic light turned red. He had to stay there with Leonard watching him. He could see the beefy face still turned in his direction. Leonard knew that in the normal course of events Brian would not have been driving through Valley Center at that hour of the day. But why should he stiffen and then stare? A neighborly wave of the hand would have been normal. Not this. Something was going on.

Brian looked up at the light. Still red. Unconsciously he shifted his hand on the steering wheel and noticed that it left a damp spot. He was too conscious of the fact that he was out looking for his daughter's killer, and Leonard was staring at him, and he was letting the whole thing get to him. But why was Leonard staring?

At last the sidelights turned amber. Then red. The traffic began to move. He jerked forward. On the edge of his vision he saw a car appear at the service entrance to Scalzo Motors. He drove on, past Burger King and the skating rink. He left Valley Center and was out on the darkening highway.

115

One by one, the cars that had been in back of him dropped away. He thought about Leonard, watching. In the rearview mirror, a pair of headlights appeared. He rounded a bend and the lights were lost. Suddenly they were there again, closing the distance. He checked to be sure his own lights were on so the car wouldn't ram him at the speed it was traveling. He expected it to pass him. Instead, the car bore down on him until it was directly in back, and then it stayed there.

He looked in the mirror. He thought it might be the same car that had come out of Scalzo Motors, but he probably only imagined it. He hadn't really seen that car.

They were on a straight section of road and there was no traffic coming the other way. The car could have passed him but it didn't. It was close enough so that its lights glared in through his back window. Again his hands felt hot on the wheel. He felt a rush of heat all over his body. He was in the middle of nowhere, on a long, dark, empty highway with mountains on both sides. The middle of nowhere.

Knock it off, he told himself. There was nothing personal in this. Just some nutty kid. Still, Leonard must have guessed what he was doing that day, and it was in Leonard's house that Patty had died. But this was not Leonard's white car.

A truck roared past in the other direction, adding more dizzying lights. He looked to the side of the road and kept his wheel steady. Sixty miles an hour. Let the bastard pass him if it wasn't fast enough. He tilted his rearview mirror to deflect its lights. It made them look farther away. He should have thought of it sooner.

The dusk was fading into darkness. On either side, the mountains rose black against a deep azure sky. Occasionally he saw lights in the distance, but most of the road was lonely. Miles of it. He checked his gas gauge. Half a tank left. The lights continued to bathe him. Made him a sitting duck. For what? He couldn't even tell how many people were in the car. All he could see were its headlights.

Four more miles. How could they keep it up so long? Four

miles to the trailer park. But he wouldn't go in. Two miles after that to the village. Maybe the guy lived in Pine Glen. But why this?

Every bend in the road was familiar. He knew that around two more bends he would come to the park. In between bends, the car could have passed him. Instead, it stayed glued to his tail, its lights shining in on him like monstrous eyes.

One more bend. Through the trees, he could see the post lamps shining. If the person was really following him, knew who he was, he probably expected him to turn in there. Brian sped past it and the car stayed with him.

Only two more miles. He passed a farm on his right and a bare field on his left. A field where they grew corn in the summer. He remembered how Patty liked corn and hadn't been able to eat it when she lost her front teeth. It was over for her now, all the things she enjoyed. Damn it, he thought.

He reached the speed zone and slowed to forty miles an hour. Here, there were houses all around him. He drove another quarter of a mile to the traffic light. It was red. The other car pulled up behind him, almost touching him. He tilted his mirror down, but he couldn't see anything.

The light turned green. He deliberately waited until that moment to put on his signal light. As soon as he began his left turn, the car followed him. Then a quick right signal and he stopped in front of the police barracks. As the car drove past, light from the drugstore fell on the driver. It was Henry Aiken, watching him.

"Good God," said Brian, and began to laugh. Henry drove on down the street and parked in front of the market. Brian stopped laughing. Henry was jealous enough to risk both their lives. It wasn't funny. But it was funnier than the cyanide killer.

He got out of his car and went into the barracks. Investigator Lou Fiedler sat alone at his desk, studying a batch of photographs.

"How's it going, Lonergan?"

"That's what I came to ask you people," Brian said.

"Still waiting for a break, I'm afraid."

"*Waiting* for a break?"

"You know what I mean. We're looking and waiting. Something's got to give sometime."

"So you don't know any more than you did two weeks ago when my daughter died."

"Yes, we do. Right after your daughter died, we didn't even know it was the sugar. Now we can trace the perpetrator's path."

"Pine Glen to Valley Center. That's not so hard."

"More than that. We've got this random pattern now. Before Cardo, it could have been just the Freaneys involved."

Brian remembered that face watching him from the showroom window. Maybe the Freaneys were more involved than anyone thought.

"I know all about that," he said.

"Right. But it started in Pine Glen. We're still concentrating on that."

"Only that?"

"Hell, no. I said concentrating, not limiting. We're working with the Valley Center police. They've got a lot of resources, as well as three murders. They've got the hospital, the poison center. And there are a couple of psychologists we've been talking to. You'd be surprised how much they can tell about a person just from the crimes he commits."

"What good does that do?" Brian asked. "You haven't even got the person."

"It helps us get him. Helps us narrow down who we're looking for."

"You going to go around and give psychological tests to everybody in the area?"

"That's not a bad idea," said Lou. "Unfortunately, we just can't do it that way."

"So what are you looking for? Tell me."

118

"A loner. Have a seat." Lou gestured toward a folding chair next to his desk.

"We're talking about a mass killer," he went on, "but it's not the kind of mass killer that grabs a rifle, runs out in the street and starts shooting people. We're talking about the sort of guy who plans and prepares it all very carefully, sets his trap, then goes home and waits to hear about it on the news. It takes a special kind of personality to do it that way. It's aggressive, but it's calculated, and he doesn't have to be on the scene. Doesn't have to watch. The guy's angry, but he has all the time in the world."

"Angry at what?" Brian asked. "What does he do it for?"

"Could be anything. He's got some kind of grievance. Could be grocery stores, consumers. Maybe his mother, or society. The guy's not rational. Maybe he can't get at the person he's really mad at. Maybe his mother's dead. It's a fantasy."

"It doesn't make sense."

"Who said it makes sense? That's why we called in the psychologists. To the killer it makes sense, but if there was any logic that the rest of us could see, we'd probably have the guy by now."

"So my kid had to die because some creep is mad at his mother?"

"I guess a lot of people have died for that kind of reason," Lou said sadly. "There's this original anger, see, and that gets buried and then it pops out at somebody else. Maybe it's not his mother, that's only a guess, but they tell me a lot of people get screwed up way back at the start, because they don't get the love they need from their mothers. And maybe they don't even know it's the mother they're angry at. It's safer to take it out on somebody else."

"Oh, God," said Brian.

"I'm just telling you what they told me. You asked."

Brian thought about it. The anger. Not being loved. Theresa had not been loved. Her mother hadn't wanted her,

119

had dumped her into a foster home, but Theresa wasn't like that. She had her problems, but he didn't think she was angry.

"A loner?" he said. "That's all?"

"Basically a loner, most likely, and there's a few other things. Probably paranoid. Hypersensitive. Isolated. Probably not many friends, if any. Maybe low self-esteem. But smart. It's pretty obvious he knows something about chemistry. And chances are he seems like a fairly normal person on the surface. Maybe a little odd, but probably seems to be leading a normal life."

"You keep saying 'he.'"

"That's just a catchall term," Lou said with a wry smile. "You want me to say he-or-she every time? Shove it."

"You mean there's a chance it could be a woman?"

"There's a chance it could be anybody, even you or me. That's just a general profile of the most likely kind of person, male or female, okay?"

"Okay. Thanks, Lou."

"I didn't tell you anything confidential, now, did I? That's the sort of stuff you could print in the paper. In fact, it probably will be in the paper."

"Why? So everybody can watch out for paranoid loners? Anybody who's a little offbeat, who had a rotten childhood?"

"Because the public has a right to know. Not so everybody can start reporting their neighbors. We're all a little bit screwy. There's no law against screwy. Who were you thinking of?"

"Nobody in particular. Hey, tell me something. Isn't it true that most people who abuse their children were probably abused by their own parents?"

"That's often the case. Why?"

"So maybe somebody who takes it out on his wife and kids—maybe he had parents who wouldn't win any prizes?"

"Could be. What are you getting at?"

"I have this neighbor—"

120

"And he abuses his kids? Real abuse? Has he ever been reported?"

"Not that I know of. It's not so much beating, but he does that sometimes. He calls it discipline."

"There's legal limits. What else?"

"The other night he locked his kid out in the cold. He's always running them down, making fun of them in front of people. He takes the boy hunting when it makes him sick. He shot a dog once, thinking it was a deer. When the boy cried about it, he called him a fag and forced him to skin the dog. It's things like that. Stuff you can't really report. He's just a mean bastard."

"Yeah, that's a tough one. Psychological abuse is tough."

"I just wondered," said Brian, "since the original box of sugar was found in his house."

"You're talking about Freaney?"

"Right."

"We were all over them with questions. We went over their whole house, before the Cardo death. But if it makes you happy, we haven't ruled anybody out."

"That really cheers me up," said Brian. "I'll see you, Lou. And thanks again."

"My pleasure."

16

The police had been watching Ernie Jacks for some time. They knew he dealt in drugs, but just knowing it didn't allow them to arrest him. They had to catch him in the act, or with the goods, and Ernie knew that. He knew how to keep out of sight, but even a fox can slip up, and one night Ernie did. It wasn't even one of his fancier drugs that caused him to lower his guard. It was plain old alcohol. An impromptu bachelor party for his pal Van, and then around the corner from the Erin Pub, he ran into a customer.

"I don't carry the stuff on me. You know that," Ernie said.

"You promised." The customer was shaking.

"Oh, the hell with it. Come on." Ernie jerked his head to show the way and led the quivering sucker to his car, a new black Buick parked regrettably close to a streetlamp.

"Get in," said Ernie.

The customer froze. "Where are you taking me?"

"Nowhere, man, just get in or get the hell away from me."

"Right." The customer climbed in. Ernie got in on the driver's side and reached under the seat. Bending down, he didn't see the police car coming around the corner. He looked up just as it pulled to a stop beside him.

The officer gestured to him to get out of the car. Ernie tried to think. There was a gun pointed at him. He had one of his own, but the officer had probably radioed for a backup.

122

Hell, thought Ernie as he got out of his car. You win a few, you lose a few.

He was pushed forward and made to lean against the car with his legs spread. The customer stood beside him in the same position. The officer held them that way until the backup arrived, and then frisked them. Ernie was clean, at least on his person. The customer had a knife.

Then they started on his car. And Ernie came to life. "Hey, man, you got a warrant for that?"

"Take it easy, Ernie, we've got everything we need."

"Lemme see the warrant. You can't search my car without a warrant. I've got a witness here. You can't—"

They found his revolver. Out came the handcuffs. He sagged. With a smart lawyer he might still beat it, but there would be a lot of unpleasantness beforehand. He had a witness, but who'd believe a guy like that?

Then they found the stuff. They took that, too. He was in a lot of trouble, but it was going to be even worse than he imagined.

The next morning, Jess Morehouse found a message waiting. URGENT, it said. Even as he reached for the telephone, it rang under his hand.

Lou Fiedler's voice said, "Hey, did you hear they picked up a guy last night and found cyanide in his car?"

"Where'd you get that?" asked Jess, immediately guessing what the message was about.

"They called me. It's some dealer named Ernie Jacks in Valley Center. They found the usual stuff, and then a plastic bag with cyanide in it."

"Pretty cute." Psychologically it didn't sound like their man, but it sure was interesting. Drug dealers were not usually in the habit of carrying cyanide. That was for a different market. "I'll keep you posted." Jess dialed the Valley Center police.

Ernie was still at the police station when Jess arrived. They had kept him up all night. He wanted to sleep like never before.

"Claims he doesn't know how the cyanide got there," said one of the interrogating officers. He turned back to Ernie. "You keep your car locked, don't you?"

"Sure I keep my car locked, but anybody can bust into a car. Or it could have happened somewheres else. How do I know?"

"Somewheres else?"

"In my house or someplace. I don't keep that stuff in my car."

"We're not talking about your house, Ernie. You had a lot of stuff in your car."

"Okay, but I didn't put it there. In my business, you get a lot of enemies. Somebody has it in for me. It's a frame. If you guys can't figure that out—"

Jess said, "Ask him what he's been doing the last three weeks."

Ernie grew sullen. "They already asked me. I been in Florida. Fort Lauderdale."

"What were you doing there?"

"I've got a woman there. Jeez, ain't anything private?"

"How long were you there?"

"Shit, I don't know. A month, month and a half. You guys should know. You been watching me."

"It's the truth," said one of the officers. "Least he wasn't here."

"When did you get back?" asked Jess.

"Wednesday."

"Which Wednesday?"

"Last Wednesday. Last week."

"How did you travel?"

"In my car. I got gas receipts. You wanna see my gas receipts?"

"Later. What's your girl friend's name and address?"

"Damn you, keep her outta this, will you?"

"She's already in it, just from knowing you. What's her

124

name, address, phone number? Where does she work?"

"Aw, come on, don't drag her in it. She's a classy chick."

"Yeah, real class. I like her friends. You want to go to jail?"

"I'm already in jail."

"We could think up some more charges. How about suspicion of homicide?"

"You can't—"

"Wanna bet?"

The telephone rang. The officer who answered it grimaced as he listened. Hanging up, he looked around at the others with a slow, sheepish grin, then turned to Ernie.

"Okay, fella, you're off the homicide hook, anyway."

"Told you," said Ernie.

"But not the drug charge, so make yourself comfortable. You're not going anywhere yet."

"What happened?" asked Jess.

Again the sheepish grin. "That was the lab. It wasn't cyanide. I guess we're all jumpy these days."

"Yeah," said Ernie self-righteously. "Jumping to conclusions."

"Okay, big time, but it wasn't any Sweet 'N Low. It's still enough to put you in jail."

The news of Ernie's capture reached the media long before the lab report was out. At Reynolds Home Center, three people told Brian that the killer had been caught.

"I know, I heard the radio, too," he said. "But it doesn't figure."

"What doesn't?" asked Joe Williams.

"A guy like that. What would he get out of it?"

"What would anybody get out of it?"

"You're right," said Brian. "But with some people, they think they're getting something out of it. This guy—I think he's just too straight."

"Too *straight?*"

"Psychologically. I don't know much about it, but it doesn't sound right to me."

"Anybody can be nuts," argued Joe.

"It's a certain kind of nuts. Somebody explained it to me, but I can't explain it. All I know is, this doesn't sound right."

At lunchtime, Brian bought a sandwich and a carton of coffee and drove to a meadow at the end of the road. He needed to think. He was beginning to feel the killer. What he had told Joe Williams that morning helped to crystallize in his own mind some of the things Lou Fiedler had said.

He felt the aloneness, the isolation. The guy was out of touch. Maybe that in itself helped him to build up fantasies about who he was killing and what he was accomplishing.

The aloneness. The man had to be his own audience. He had to be content that only he would know how clever he had been.

And he had been clever. Even Brian had to give him that. He not only needed to know about chemistry, he also had to avoid being detected.

Alone. Angry—but quietly angry. Intelligent, possibly educated—but off the wall. Probably not even aware that he was off the wall. How many people are aware of it? Only when it begins to interfere with the way they see their lives.

The crimes had begun in Pine Glen. Brian knew many of the people there. The majority, perhaps. But Pine Glen might only have been a diversion. The real Ground Zero might have been Valley Center, which was much larger. Brian had grown up near there, had gone to school in Valley Center, but there was no reason to think the killer was of his generation.

It could have been anybody. But he would start with what he knew. He would continue to feel the killer. Feel what he was thinking, doing, where he was. It sounded crazy, but he could not get over the idea that there was some kind of bond between them, because of Patty. The killer would be thinking about him, too.

17

Theresa struggled for breath as the earth covered her face. She tried to twist and turn, to fight her way out, but the weight of the sand would not let her move. She screamed and no one heard her. Sand filled her mouth, her nostrils. It gritted in her eyes. She kicked and flailed her arms, but they wouldn't move. Again and again she tried to scream. Every time she took a breath to scream, more sand filled her throat. The horror . . . the horror . . .

"Theresa!"

She was rocked awake. She lay gasping, her face free of sand. In her room. With Brian. She could see him on his elbow, looming over her. He was holding her shoulder and shaking her.

"What happened? My God!"

"A . . . dream," she managed to say. She still could not believe she was breathing air.

"You acted as if you were suffocating."

"I was. Buried alive."

"Not again. Did you have that dream again?"

"It was more." Gradually she was able to catch her breath. She remembered having the dream before. It had made her think of Patty. "Not Patty this time. It was—me."

"You?"

"I dreamt I was little. And—" She could hardly say it, even to Brian—"dreamt they raped me."

"Who?"

"Big boys. They raped me."

"How little were you in the dream? A child?"

"I think so. A child. They raped— And I told on them. But nobody believed me. They put me in a dark room."

"That's because Mrs. Sentry used to do that. That's why you dreamed it."

"Mrs. Sentry. Yes, it was Mrs. Sentry."

"In your dream?"

"I didn't see her, but—yes. She'd do that. She said I was dirty to say those things. Then the boys got mad. They buried me alive. A big sand—like a mountain."

"Why would you dream a thing like that, Theresa?"

"I don't know."

"Do you think maybe it really happened?"

"I don't remember it."

"Maybe you remember it in your subconscious."

"But a thing like that—wouldn't I remember?"

"Maybe not, if you didn't want to. You said there's a lot of blanks. It's probably things that got so rough you closed the door on it."

"Why would I dream about it now?"

"Well, you're under a lot of stress."

"I thought dreams were usually disguised. In symbols."

"Then maybe it's a symbol for something else. Anyway, you're okay now."

"Not really."

"It can't have actually happened, or you'd be dead, wouldn't you?"

"I don't know. I'm sure I'd remember something like that, if it happened. But it seemed so horribly real."

"Does it now? Sometimes dreams seem real while they're going on, but afterward you can see how crazy they are."

"It still does. I felt it. I felt the sand. And I was so scared."

128

"It's all over now," he said again.

He held her for a while longer and then fell asleep with his arm under her head.

She lay awake, afraid to sleep. She might have the dream again. It had felt so real, she might even suffocate just from dreaming it. In any case, she couldn't stand the fear.

She eased herself away from him and sat up. She couldn't risk falling asleep. She would spend the rest of the night in the living room, watching television.

Michael saw her turn on the set. She thought she wouldn't fall asleep, but she did. He switched it off.

He had heard her tell about the dream. He wondered what had brought it on. Maybe she was still thinking of Patty. Maybe she couldn't handle the idea of her child being dead, and thought of her as alive. Buried alive. It must have been a horrible dream. But better than the reality. He could imagine her relief at waking up in the clear air.

In a little while he was ready to leave. He went out, pushed the snap lock on the door and pulled it closed as quietly as he could. It was five o'clock in the morning. He had about an hour. Not much time.

There was very little traffic on the Quickway. If there had been more, he could have driven faster without attracting attention. He had about twenty miles to go and twenty miles back, most of it on the Quickway. It was not too bad.

But then there were five miles on a winding mountain road. He had clocked it on an earlier trip. But that had been daytime, and he wasn't able to do much exploring around the plant.

He saw the night lights on when he arrived. Pale, cold fluorescents, shining through the windows. There was a night watchman, too, but he knew how to avoid the man.

He left his car far enough away so the watchman wouldn't hear him closing the door, and then he went around to a side window and boosted himself up so he could see inside.

129

Big drums of chemicals were stacked against the wall. He stared in fascination. Fascinated with his own ingenuity in finding this place. Hwy Metal Works, it was called. He supposed the Hwy stood for Highway, even though it was far off the beaten path. He had found it after reading about cyanide in the encyclopedia. He read that it was used in processing metals. Electroplating. Casehardening. Precipitating gold and silver from their ores.

He had no idea what Hwy's specialty was, and didn't really care. All that interested him were those drums of chemicals stacked against the wall.

Theresa woke. The television set was off. She remembered turning it on. She felt the familiar lump of dread in her chest. But when she sat up and looked into the ashtray, it was clean and empty.

She hadn't meant to sleep. At least she hadn't had the dream again. She couldn't remember dreaming at all.

It was almost six-thirty. Brian would be getting up. She could have breakfast with him. Too often she had lain in bed. He would get tired of her. She couldn't lose him, too.

He woke when she went into the bedroom. He stared at her groggily. "What are you doing up already?"

"I didn't want to sleep again after that dream," she said.

"That was rough, honey."

She sat down on the bed. He slipped his arms around her. "Don't you think maybe you should talk to somebody about it? You'll drive yourself crazy."

She twisted away from him. "You keep talking as if I'm sick! I know what's wrong, and there's nothing a doctor can do about it. He can't bring back my child."

She had said the wrong thing, and she had said it before. He was losing patience with her.

"You've got to face reality, hon. There's nothing that's going to bring her back. The only thing you can change is how you live with it."

"You don't understand," she told him with a whimper.

130

"I do understand. She was my kid too. I'm as heartbroken as you are, but facts are facts." He stood up and began to get out his clothes for work. He continued to look sharp, while she was sinking farther and farther into chronic depression. He added in almost an undertone, "Maybe she was only meant to live eight years."

"You can't believe that!"

"I don't know what I believe. I only know that she's gone and we're still here, and that's the way it is. Maybe you were too involved with her, if—"

"Involved with her? I'm her mother! What are you talking about?"

"You didn't let me finish. I was trying to say, maybe you poured your whole life into her, and now that she's gone, there's nothing left of you."

"Maybe."

"But you're a separate person, Theresa."

"I don't think you understand what it's like to be a mother."

"I guess I don't. Only a father."

"You could have other children." She stopped at the look on his face. A startled, stricken look. He went into the bathroom without saying anything further.

She curled up on the bed, knowing she should go out to the kitchen and start the coffee. "Wallowing in self-pity." Was she doing that? She should have been thinking of him. It was his grief, too. But she couldn't imagine a father being as involved as a mother. She had borne the child. Lived for her. And for what? Only eight years. As Brian had once said, there was supposed to be a whole lifetime.

For whom? For Patty or herself? She was feeling sorry for herself, for being cheated out of Patty's growing up, and out of her grandchildren.

But she had had Patty for eight delightful years. Some people never had a child.

She decided, bitterly, that she would rather have been childless than go through this.

She heard Brian's electric shaver. A moment later he

131

turned it off and came out of the bathroom. He sat down beside her on the bed and took her hand.

"Honey, I'm sorry. When I said you're a separate person, I should remember that you're a separate person from me, too. I can't expect you to deal with things the same way I do."

"I don't understand," she replied, "how you can not care."

He withdrew his hand and let it fall. "What do you mean not care?"

Again she had said the wrong thing. She was so constantly on the edge of tears that once more she began to cry.

He said, "Now you're judging me by the way you handle things. You're doing exactly what I was doing."

"I'm sorry. I don't—I can't—"

"Okay, we're both sorry. I'll tell you what. We can—Even though we miss her, we can have a different kind of life now. How about if we go out tonight?"

"Go out?"

"I thought we might have dinner."

He wanted to. This was her chance to do something he wanted, instead of staying at home and being miserable, but she wasn't sure she could handle it.

"I don't want anybody to see me," she said.

"They won't. We can go to Little Bavaria up on the back road. At least it won't be full of people we know."

She would have to handle it. And keep on handling it for the rest of her life. She had not thought much about the rest of her life, but she knew she couldn't lose Brian.

"What are you going to do today?" he asked later, as he was leaving for work.

"Maybe clean the house."

"Theresa, the house is already clean. Why don't you go shopping, or something?"

"Shopping? For what?"

"Anything. Enjoy yourself. Go to a movie. Or come down and have lunch with me."

"But if we're going out to dinner . . ."

132

"Okay, lunch next week. But start living again, Theresa, please?"

Living? That had been Patty.

"I'll try," she said.

After he left she washed the breakfast dishes, then stood at the kitchen window looking out at the road. At Cheryl's house. It was yellow, with that big bay window in the front, and a gabled roof. It looked more like a house than a trailer. It was a nice house, and Cheryl still had her family. Both her children.

She also had Leonard. In that respect, Theresa was the more fortunate. But if she could have Patty back . . .

Her mind was caught on Leonard. She couldn't think past him. Even before she knew him, she hadn't liked him. It had struck her from the moment she first met him. Something— terrible.

She turned from the window and went to straighten the bedroom.

Brian asked her that evening what she had done during the day.

"I went to the mall in Valley Center," she said, "but I didn't buy anything."

"Good. Did you have a nice time?"

"I don't know. Just a time. It wasn't either nice or not nice."

She was glad he believed her. The truth was, she didn't know what she had done. She couldn't explain it any more than she could the other times it had happened. All of a sudden it had been four o'clock and she was turning in at their driveway. She had been driving the car without knowing it.

This time she remembered to check the odometer. She wasn't sure what it had read that morning, but thought she must have put on about forty miles. Driven forty miles in a blackout. Somehow, she had been able to do it. Somewhere, she must have been conscious.

133

What if someone saw her? Someone she knew? What if they remembered and she didn't?

"Ready to go?" asked Brian.

She had forgotten about dinner.

"I guess so."

She did not want to go. She wanted to be left alone to think, but she couldn't disappoint him and she couldn't do anything to make him suspicious.

"Let me change first."

"You're okay," he called after her as she went to the bedroom. She was not okay in jeans, when he looked so elegant in his tan suede jacket. She put on gray wool slacks and a pink tailored shirt.

Her face looked pale and ravaged. A little makeup would help. Eye makeup and blusher, and rosy lipstick. It brought her up to par. Now maybe they wouldn't stare at her and know that she was the women whose child had died. What if the killer was somewhere around, watching?

As they got into Brian's car, Theresa glanced over at the Freaneys' house and saw a curtain pulled aside in the living room.

"Cheryl's watching us," she said.

"Let her. She doesn't know where we're going," Brian replied.

"That's the sort of thing I hate. People being curious about us."

"Maybe she's concerned."

"I don't want that, either. I just want to be invisible."

She stared out at the dark night, remembering that ride in the ambulance. They were on the same road.

How many times since then had she driven it and not known? It gave her a feeling of sick dread. She wanted to be invisible. Instead, she was the one who couldn't see, while others could see her.

Brian turned off the main road onto a narrower one that climbed the mountain. Isolated houses twinkled in the night and bungalow colonies, closed for the winter, stood like small ghost towns against the bare trees and winter sky.

And then, around a bend, they came to Little Bavaria, a bright oasis in the midst of darkness. Its entire roof was outlined in colored lights. Flood lamps, hidden among the shrubs, lit the entrance. Brian took her elbow and guided her inside as though she couldn't walk by herself.

The interior, too, was bright. She could have wished for dimmer lights, but no one paid attention to them as they were led to a table in a far corner, against the wall. Brian had known she would like that. She made an effort to act interested in the occasion because it was what he wanted, but she was not doing well. She had almost forgotten how to talk to him, except about Patty.

And there was the nagging thought that they were enjoying themselves at Patty's expense. She tried to hold it back, but after he had ordered, she burst out, "Do you realize we never could have done this before without a baby-sitter?"

She watched a muscle twitch in his cheek. Then he said, "I know. And we aren't going to be able to do anything or go anywhere without thinking of her. We just can't help it. Even if we stayed home."

Especially if they stayed home, was what he meant.

She tried hard to think of something to talk about. Anything. But there was nothing beyond the central fact of Patty.

Finally she said, "I'm not much fun, am I?"

"About as much as I am," he replied.

"I keep thinking, some people can have a good life together, just as a couple. But they—haven't lost—" She shouldn't have said it. Now she would start to cry right there in the restaurant, and their evening would be ruined.

She managed to control herself. Gradually the teary feeling subsided. She tried to listen as Brian talked about his work. He was only doing it to take her mind off Patty.

Suddenly his expression changed. She caught it for only a moment, the unguarded surprise. She looked around.

135

"It's Dorian," she said.

"And Henry Aiken. She calls him Hank."

She saw the way Dorian looked at Brian. They had once had an affair, and Dorian was single. That look told a lot.

"Sort of sad, the way he keeps after her," Brian was saying. "At least, if he weren't so crazy. The guy's a real nut."

"Who?"

"Henry." He nodded toward the pair, who had taken a table across the room.

"What about it?"

"She keeps turning him down. He gets pretty upset about it. She even thought he might be the one who tampered with the sugar in her store, out of spite. That was before Valley Center."

Now that they were seated, she couldn't see them very well. Brian's words came spottily.

"—even went up to Valley Center to talk to him. Remember that time?"

"I think so." It seemed a safe answer. She wasn't really listening. Dorian was available. By her, he could have other children.

"Do you still like her?" she asked.

"Who? Her? That was years ago. Before I met you."

"Why didn't you marry her?"

"She wanted to go to New York and be a model."

"But then she came back."

"Didn't make it. Just another small-town girl with a dream."

He hadn't said he didn't want to marry her.

Their dinner arrived. For a while, they ate in silence. From time to time, Brian's eyes were drawn to the other couple. As often as not, he caught Henry watching him. He wondered if Henry really had it in for him, or had only been upset that night on the highway. With a guy like Henry, you couldn't tell. Brian hoped he didn't own a handgun.

He wondered what it meant, the two of them going out

together. Maybe she had reconsidered. Although it appeared not, from the way Henry looked at him.

"You talked to her, didn't you?" Theresa asked.

"What do you mean?"

"It started in her store. But you already talked to her, and so did the police."

"That was before—"

His brain reeled. He had thought of it earlier. About Dorian. Now it hit him again. The fact that it had started in her store. Maybe the rest had been a cover-up.

But he had been over it before. And rejected it, because it was all so accidental. Still, the police might have had it wrong. They could only guess at what must have happened, and maybe they were wrong. Could Dorian have done that terrible thing to Patty, to get Brian to marry her and have the family he has lost? Not Dorian!

It did seem incredible. After all, she was someone he knew. But then it began to seem less incredible. She had certainly gone after him. She had offered Cliff and herself.

Or maybe it was Henry. Maybe all of Valley Center had been a cover-up. Maybe that crazy night on the highway had had nothing to do with Dorian or jealousy, but the fact that Brian was prowling around, looking for the killer.

"What's the matter, Brian?"

He caught himself quickly. "Nothing. I'm not immune to it, either, you know. I get moments."

She looked down at her plate. "I guess I mostly think of myself."

"It's natural. You were pretty close to her." He could afford to be generous with her now, and she with him.

"We both were. And you were a good father."

He winced.

"It's not fair," she went on. "Leonard Freaney's a terrible father, and he gets to keep his children."

That was where they kept ending up. At the Freaneys'. That was where the first poisoned sugar had been found.

But it might have been one of the others. It might have been Cardo. Did she have any money? He couldn't believe Jennie would do a thing like that, but you never could tell.

Or someone in Valley Center. Maybe Pine Glen was the cover-up.

"I wonder," he said, "if the whole thing was deliberate."

"Of course it was. They ruled out an accident."

"I mean—"

She looked up at him, and he was surprised at what he saw in her eyes. Bleak fear.

18

"Brian, didja see the paper?"

Joe Williams thrust a copy of the *Journal* at him, even before Brian had a chance to take off his coat. The word CYANIDE leaped up and hit him.

"Village police received an anonymous tip yesterday that a Valley Center man was hiding cyanide in his home. Police searched a third-floor apartment on Willow Avenue which is rented to 29-year-old Boyd Wentz and found a large cache of chemicals, many potentially dangerous. Among them was a plastic bottle filled with cyanide. Wentz, who works in the Service Division at Scalzo Motors, claims to be an amateur chemist whose hobby is experimenting with various substances. He told police he was trying to develop an artificial fuel for automobiles."

"Artificial fuel, huh?" Joe said as he leaned over Brian's shoulder. "You need cyanide for that?"

It was something else that had caught Brian's attention. "Scalzo Motors. That's where my neighbor works."

"The guy that had the poisoned sugar?" As soon as he said it, Joe was embarrassed. They tried not to mention Patty, even indirectly.

"That's the one."

"Sodium cyanide," Joe said, looking further into the article.

139

"That's salt!" exclaimed an early customer who had been examining a display of door locks. "Isn't that salt?"

"No," said Haskin Jones, pausing in his daily, self-assigned task of spraying the telephones with disinfectant, "salt is sodium chloride."

"Yeah?" said the customer.

Brian took the newspaper into his boss's empty office and reread the article. There it was in black and white. Scalzo Motors.

He didn't know what it meant. All it said to him immediately was that the Freaneys knew someone who owned the cyanide. The police had taken Wentz in for questioning, but they hadn't arrested him. At least they had found him, for whatever that was worth.

He looked up to find Joe watching him. "Interesting?" asked Joe, as quietly proud as though he had cracked the whole case.

"It is," said Brian. "We'll have to see what comes of it."

It sounded more interesting than the drug pusher, who hadn't even been around when the poisonings took place.

That evening, he showed the article to Theresa. She had already seen it. She had read the whole paper, but did not seem particularly impressed.

"It doesn't prove anything," she said.

"Of course it doesn't prove anything," Brian replied, "but don't you get the connection with Scalzo Motors?"

"So? You think this man tried to poison Leonard? To get his job, maybe?"

"Now you're being silly. Except he might have had a reason."

Maybe Leonard was messing with the man's wife. Or the man was after Cheryl. But he might just as easily have gotten Cheryl. Or the children.

He did not voice any more of his thoughts. Theresa seemed to be more concerned about something else, and she wouldn't tell him what it was.

***

After he had gone to bed that night, Brian lay awake for a long time, thinking. Finally he got up and went out to the living room.

It was icy cold. They always turned down the thermostat at night. He could have turned it up now, but the furnace was noisy and he was afraid of waking her.

He went to the kitchen window and looked out at the Freaneys' house. If only he could feel it more clearly. But maybe the box that had been there was not the original one. Maybe that had been a cover-up, and the target was somewhere else. Or maybe it was all random and there was no special target.

Still, he couldn't get over the coincidence that Leonard had a friend with cyanide. He looked at their house for a long time, trying to absorb the feel of it. Trying to sense what had happened.

Their windows were dark. All the Freaneys were asleep. Only the post lamp was on, and an amber light burning at the front door. He wondered why they had left their front door light on all night.

He closed his eyes and tried to feel. He had never even thought of such a thing before, of trying to pick up vibrations, or thought waves. People talked about things like that. It made a certain amount of sense. He should be able to tune in. He was using clichés. But it all made sense.

What was the killer thinking now? Had he achieved what he set out to do?

"Are you happy now?" he asked. "Did you get what you wanted?"

He waited. He was beginning to feel something. A kind of block. An uneasiness. He worked on it, but he was pushing too hard. He couldn't tell any more what might have come from outside and what was in his own mind. But something, he thought, had come from somewhere.

He jumped at a sound in the living room. He turned and was startled to find Theresa there, watching him.

"What are you doing?" he asked. "Sleepwalking?"

"No." Her voice was husky and she seemed to be angry about something. Hostile. "I wondered what you were doing," she said.

"I'm thinking."

"About what?"

"The killings. Sometimes if you just let your mind float for a while . . ."

"That's not how they usually do it," she said, probably meaning the police.

"I've got to know who it is."

"And then?" She folded her arms and gave him a straight, bold stare that was not like her at all.

"I told you, I don't know." He hadn't thought much about that yet. He just wanted the killer.

"It must be somebody around here," he added lamely.

"I wouldn't be surprised."

"They ought to be able to get some kind of lead."

"It's not that easy, when the killer didn't have any contact with the victims, never got anywhere near them."

"But maybe he did. I've been thinking about it. I— Sit down, Theresa."

"I'm not—"

"Do you want some coffee?"

"No." She seemed restless, but she took a seat at the dining table. He pulled out a chair and sat opposite her.

"What if it was more intentional than they think?" he said. "Not Patty and not Marylou, but what if that box of sugar— what if it was poisoned after it got to the Freaneys'?"

"Why do you say that?"

"And the rest might be a cover-up. Otherwise they'd be concentrating on the Freaneys. Without the cover-up, I mean. Which is maybe where they should be concentrating."

"Why would anybody try to poison the Freaneys?" she asked.

"All right, maybe one of the others. I just thought of the Freaneys because of that Scalzo connection, and because Leonard's the kind of guy who gets carried away."

142

"I don't think poisoning is his style."

"No, I guess he's more apt to bludgeon."

"On the other hand . . ." She tilted her head thoughtfully. "He can get awfully vindictive."

"So he could premeditate."

"But I think he'd get more satisfaction out of watching the actual death."

She said it without flinching. He was surprised.

"If it was right there in his own house, he could watch," Brian said.

"But who in his own house? He acts as if he hates them all, but most guys like that just run away. Or maybe Cheryl. Do you think he's fooling around on the side? I wouldn't be surprised."

"It's worth looking into," he said.

"How are you going to do that?"

"I'll think about it. I really feel I've gotten somewhere tonight. Even if it turns out to be the wrong track."

"Yes, you have. Why don't you run off to bed now?"

"How about both of us?" he suggested.

"Not me for a while. I've had my shut-eye."

He couldn't understand the way she was talking. It wasn't Theresa at all. Her whole manner was different. It was as though she had gotten over Patty, suddenly and completely. Maybe even gotten over being herself.

He took another look out of the window. "I wish there were some way I could bug their house."

"Do you know how to do that?"

"No, but I could probably find out."

"It's illegal, anyway," she reminded him.

"So is murder."

He hesitated before he started back down the hall, to see if she would go with him. She seemed to be waiting for him to leave. He wondered what she was doing. It worried him, but he had no right to spy on her. All he knew was, she was acting healthier than she had in a long time, and he didn't want to do anything to change that.

He got into bed and lay on his back, thinking. The windows with their white curtains formed gray rectangles in the night. Five rectangles. It was a nice room.

He thought about the Freaneys. He wished he knew what went on there. Sometimes he did know, when they exploded into shouts and screams. Or when he was over there and Leonard started picking on Cheryl, or both of them picked at the kids.

Maybe it wasn't the Freaneys at all. Maybe one of the others. He was back to that, and the police would have told him to let them handle it. But they never seemed to get anywhere.

And he had one thing the police didn't have. He had the Freaneys right across the road where he could watch them.

Cheryl felt a burning in her stomach. She wondered if she might be getting an ulcer. Was that what an ulcer felt like? She didn't even know.

He was out there again. Brian Lonergan. He pretended to be working on his car, getting it ready for winter, but there were long periods when he would lean against the radiator grill and watch her house. Before that, he had been inside at his kitchen window, watching.

If she stayed away from the bay window, he wouldn't see her. She went back to the kitchen and began scrubbing the sink. But she dropped the can of cleanser, spraying powder all over the floor.

"Oh-h-h," she wept, stifling her outcry so Leonard wouldn't hear.

"What happened?" asked Bonnie, coming into the kitchen.

Cheryl clenched her teeth and clasped her hands between her knees as she bent over the mess. It was the only way she knew of to keep from hitting the child. She wished they would all go, damn it, all go to the rifle range with Leonard.

Bonnie was still there, watching her.

"Go to your room," Cheryl said in a tight voice. Bonnie recognized the voice, and fled down the hall. At least she knew when to stay out of the way, which was more than you could say for Mark.

Cheryl swept up the powder, but some of it had gotten wet and she had to mop it. She heard Mark's voice at the end of the hall, protesting. And Leonard: "Damned little fag, get your shoes on and get out there."

"I have homework." Mark sounded high and whiny. His voice hadn't changed yet.

"Don't give me that homework talk. You're too dumb to get through school anyway. You're too dumb for anything. Can't even shoot a gun. Now get out there!"

Cheryl rested against the sink. The pain felt like a knife piercing her gut. And it was new. She had never had it until the last few days. It was Brian's fault, the way he watched her. He was angry about Patty. Angry because they couldn't find the killer. He blamed her. She blamed herself. She should have given Patty that drink of Coke. Maybe if she'd paid more attention, she could have saved her.

"But I didn't know," she murmured to the window.

"What are you mumbling about?" She hadn't heard Leonard come into the kitchen. "You crazy, talking to yourself?"

"I just don't feel well," she said.

"Lazy, huh? You're a lazy slob."

She knew better than to argue with those remarks. As soon as he left, she would go and lie down.

She couldn't tell him about Brian. He would say it was her fault. She wished they were all dead.

The thought surprised her so much that she clamped her hand to her mouth. She turned to see whether Leonard had read her mind, but he was busy prodding Mark out the door. Mark's head was bowed and he was sullen. He didn't even look back at her. She remembered the thing about the dog last year. That was too much. Leonard shouldn't have done that.

Another knife zeroed in on her and she sat down in a chair, clutching at her stomach. A tear rolled down her cheek. She wiped it away in case Leonard came back.

For thirteen years she had kidded herself that they were all

146

right. Maybe a little more volatile than some families, but they were going to make it. She told herself it was nothing unusual that Leonard lost his temper sometimes. Even when he hit her, she made excuses for him. He was overwrought. She should have been a better wife. He was overly strict with the kids, but she thought that was better than spoiling them, and if she ever tried to stop him it just got worse for all of them, so she learned to keep her peace and let him handle it.

But that thing with the dog. She thought Mark had behaved abominably, crying like a baby, and she was glad she hadn't been there to see it. But Leonard . . . She hadn't realized when they told her about it. She only realized it gradually over the next year, but it made her stand back and look at him. He was incapable of loving. Only of anger. His strictness with the children was harsh and hostile. His feeling for her was lust. And dependency. He was very dependent on her, and he tried to keep her from leaving him by making her feel she wasn't worth anything on her own.

She tried telling herself that the dog thing was only one incident, and there were the good times, too. She didn't know what to do. Sometimes she loved him and other times she wished he would—die. It was the only way she could think of to get him out of her life. She could not imagine asking for a divorce.

Someone knocked at the door. She couldn't see who it was. For a moment she hoped it was Marylou Grover, the only person she could talk to, but Marylou was dead.

It was Brian. She stared at him with her mouth slightly open. She hadn't heard Leonard's car leave, but it was gone. She was alone there with Bonnie Ann.

"Hello," she said.

"Morning. Are you going to let me in?"

She stood back. He looked around as though expecting to find something, then pulled out a chair and sat down. That was her social center, the kitchen table. The living room was mostly for television.

"Getting ready for the hunting season, huh?" he asked.

"What?"

"I saw Leonard going off with the boy and some rifles."

"Yes. The practice range." She was about to offer him some coffee. But no one wanted her coffee any more, after Marylou.

Brian didn't say anything. He sat and looked at her and it made her nervous. She began twisting her fingers together. She wished she had a cigarette, but she hadn't bought any. With this stomach thing, she was trying to give them up.

Finally, because he still wouldn't speak, she asked, "How's Theresa?"

"Not so good," he said. "She's very depressed. I'm not sure a person ever gets over this kind of thing."

He watched her steadily and she knew he was blaming her. She couldn't meet his eyes. She had to look at the floor, and that made it worse.

"Do you know why I'm here?" he asked.

She wanted to say something snappy, but could only shake her head.

He said, "I read something in the paper about a mechanic at Scalzo Motors. You must know who I mean. Is he a friend of yours?"

Her mind began to reel. Of course they knew Boyd Wentz.

"He's not really a mechanic," she said. "He just sort of—"

"That's not what I wanted to know, Cheryl. I wanted to know how well you know him."

"I, uh—not too well. He's not married, see. Usually we go with couples."

She was proud of herself for thinking of that. It was true, in a way. Leonard didn't even like Boyd. He called him a fag, because Boyd was gentler and more interested in intelligent things than Leonard. And Leonard would kill them both if he ever learned that she found Boyd a sympathetic person to talk to. Not as close as Marylou had been, and there was nothing romantic about it, but she could talk to Boyd as she never could to Leonard, because Leonard never wanted to listen to anyone.

"You'd better not jump to conclusions," she said. "He hasn't been in this house in ages."

Brian smiled. "Was I jumping to conclusions?"

The smile disturbed her. She had probably said too much. He had tricked her into it. Now he knew that Boyd had been in that house at some time past.

"I wish you'd leave me alone," she said.

"I'm sure you do."

"Boyd had nothing to do with it."

"How do you know?"

Again she had said too much. She didn't know. But she couldn't believe it of Boyd.

"He really is smart," she told him. "He should have a much better job. He's real smart with chemistry and things like that, but he wouldn't hurt anybody."

"Any idea where he might have gotten the stuff?"

"What stuff?"

"What stuff do you think we're talking about, Cheryl?"

"If you mean poison, I don't think Boyd Wentz would have anything like that around."

He stared thoughtfully at the table. Probably trying to recall the newspaper article. She couldn't remember herself whether the police had actually found any cyanide in Boyd's apartment.

She added triumphantly, "Where would he get it, anyway?"

"That's what I just asked you."

Suddenly he jumped up and went into the living room. He came back with the telephone book, flipping through it as he walked. Then he stopped and ran his finger down a page.

"Ha!" he said. "One ten Willow Avenue. That's Wentz's address, right? An apartment house?"

"A two-family house," she answered dully. "He's upstairs."

"And look who's downstairs." Brian held out the book and pointed to a line. She couldn't read it from that distance.

"Frank Price," he said, noting her confusion. "I talked to him. He teaches chemistry at the high school and I happen to

149

know he had some cyanide. It must be very convenient for a chemistry buff to have a guy like Price for a neighbor."

"But Boyd wouldn't do anything like that!" she cried.

"Of course not. He was trying to develop an artificial fuel."

She caught the sarcasm, and glared at him. "He wouldn't," she insisted. "He just likes to fool around, to experiment. He told me he knew where he could get some really interesting chemicals, so I guess he meant Frank Price."

"Told you? Just you? How well do you know this guy?"

"I hardly know him. We got to talking at a party." She began to breathe again. She had pulled that one off all right. If Brian ever found out that she and the children spent time with Boyd, that he was the kind of man they wished they had in their lives, it might get back to Leonard.

"Was this an agreement with Price, or did he just take them?" Brian asked.

"Oh, I don't know," she answered angrily. "Why do you keep bugging me? You're always bugging me. Why don't you go and ask him, if you want to know?"

"I'm sure the police are asking him."

"They let him go."

She could tell from Brian's startled look that he hadn't known.

"They couldn't hold him," she went on, glad that, for once, she had caught Brian off balance. "They had nothing to hold him on."

"Of course they'll keep tabs on him."

She nodded sickly. They would. But at least they had let him go. He had called her late yesterday to tell her that. Called her when he knew Leonard wouldn't be home.

Brian leaned back in his chair. She wished he would go. She wanted to lie down. Sitting got her doubled up inside and made the pain worse.

"Do you have a nice life, Cheryl?" he asked.

"A—what?"

"A nice life. Are you happy with it?"

"I guess so. Why?"

"I just wondered. You always seem so contented."

Was he kidding her? Or maybe she did seem that way, because she was pretty good at kidding herself.

"I guess so," she said again.

"It's always interesting to know what people would wish for if they could have anything they wanted."

"That's a baby game."

"No, it isn't. We do it all our lives. It's just that kids are more open about it."

"I'll bet I know what you'd want," she said.

"Well, yes. It makes everything else seem unimportant. But what about you? Aside from the usual million dollars, isn't there anything you'd want that you don't have?"

"I guess so." If he only knew what she really wanted. "I always wished we could eat out more."

"That's important to you?"

"Well, maybe not the most important thing, but it's nice. I like to dress up a little, in a clean pair of jeans, and have somebody else do the cooking. It makes me feel special."

That was true. She really loved it. She would even have gotten a job so they could afford luxuries like that, but Leonard would have his own ideas about how to spend the money.

"What else?" Brian asked.

"Oh, I know. I'd love to have a double-wide trailer. This place is so cramped. The rooms are too small."

"Yes, that would be nice."

He sounded grim when he said it. She hadn't meant to point up the fact that they needed the room while he and Theresa did not.

"And," she went on, quickly changing the subject, "I wish Leonard and Mark would get off each other's backs."

He seemed politely interested. "What do you mean?"

"You know how they are. They're always at each other."

"And that bothers you?"

151

"Of course it does. It's so—it makes everything so—if Mark just wouldn't talk back all the time. If he didn't want to be different. Sometimes I wonder how he ever got into this family."

"I always thought it was the usual way."

"Oh, yes," she said.

"He's not adopted, is he?"

"Oh, no. But you know what I mean. With a guy like Leonard you have to—"

"You have to agree with him."

"Well, it would help, just to keep things smooth."

"And it's up to the rest of you to adjust to Leonard."

She shrugged, then let her shoulders droop. "You know how he is," she said.

"So the kids have no right to themselves. They're growing up with their own personalities and talents and interests stifled, because they have to cater to a lousy, neurotic bastard."

"Brian, just get out of here."

"I'm sorry," he said. "It gets me mad, but I didn't mean to run off about it. The guy's a stinker and he has everything." He stood up from the table, leaving her speechless. He had been angry, but she could feel his pain.

"You know something?" he said as he pulled open the door. "There had better be a heaven. There had just better be a heaven, with some justice in it."

As he crossed the road, he saw Theresa watching from the kitchen window. She met him at the door. "Where were you?"

He still felt dazed from his outburst. "You saw where I was. Over at Cheryl's."

"At *Cheryl's?*"

"Well, that's who happens to be home over there. I went to see what I could find out about the punk at Scalzo's, and I figured Cheryl's the easiest one to get to. She shakes up easily, and you can almost tell what she's thinking."

152

"I hope you had fun."

"Not really. But I found out a few things. They're friendly with the punk. He's been in their house, but if she's telling the truth, not recently. And we talked a little about their family dynamics."

"Why? You know about their family dynamics."

"I thought it might have something to do with what happened. We both know how hung-up Leonard is. I was trying to find out if he could be crazy enough to knock off his own kids."

"Why?" she asked.

"Jealousy, maybe. He might want Cheryl all to himself. Or maybe he was trying to knock Cheryl off."

Theresa turned away. She didn't really care about the killer. She only wanted Patty, and that was impossible.

"For a while last night," he said, "I thought you were starting to feel better."

"Last night?" she rubbed a hand across her forehead.

"Were you sleepwalking after all?" he asked. "You said you weren't."

"I guess I must have been."

"You seemed awake. We had a nice talk. But you didn't act like you."

"How did I act?"

"It's hard to say. More assertive, maybe. And happier."

"Then I definitely was sleepwalking."

She said it flatly, trying to end the conversation. But she was more than worried, he could see that. She was frightened.

Late in the afternoon, he took Alice for a walk. He asked Theresa to go with him, but she wasn't feeling well. He walked to the end of the park, where the woods sloped down toward Winding Creek. When they were far enough away from the houses, he unfastened Alice's leash to let her run. She crashed happily through the underbrush, chasing a squirrel. There was a path of sorts that went on to the creek, but he

153

couldn't see the creek from where he stood, even with most of the leaves gone. He could see the mountains on the other side of the valley, and Alice—

He spun around. He had felt it brush past his face at the same moment he heard the explosion.

"Hey, watch it!" he called. "That's my dog!"

At the sound of his voice, Alice came running back to him. Another shot struck a tree just above his head.

He shouted again. "Hold your fire! I'm here! What are you trying to do?"

Alice barked and began to run in circles. He flung himself on top of her and they both fell to the ground. His hand came down on a briar. Alice struggled against him but he held her tightly. It wasn't Alice they were after, he knew that now, but if she was visible, it would show them where he was.

Afterward, they could always say it was an accident. That they were target shooting and didn't know he was there. But they did know. He had become a threat.

He wondered if they could see him on the ground. He wondered if they would wait until he tried to go home, or whether they would come looking for him. The sun was still up, but it was low. He could wait there until dark. He spoke to Alice and soothed her, trying to keep her quiet. He shifted to a more comfortable position and listened for any sound that might be human.

My God, he thought as he went over it again, no one would even be suspicious. A man walking in the woods near the hunting season was taking his life into his hands. No matter that they shouldn't have been shooting so close to a residential area. They would say they had been firing into the woods and never dreamed anybody was there. Since hunters did all sorts of crazy things, no one would have any reason to doubt them.

Something rustled in the bushes above him. He tightened his grip on Alice. "Sorry, girl," he murmured. "Only a little longer." He couldn't be sure of that. They might be coming now. He listened, but didn't hear any more. The sun was just above the horizon. Soon it would go down, but he would have to wait longer for darkness.

Another rustle. He tensed. There was a boulder several feet away on his right. He would be safer if he could get behind it, but he didn't dare move.

Alice squirmed against the restraint.

"Stay down, girl, damn it."

The cold was getting to him. He began to shiver.

He turned and watched the sun. He could almost see it moving. And then it was gone.

He waited until he saw darkness begin to gather like something palpable in the air before he started home.

When he entered his house, covered with burrs and bits of leaves, Theresa looked at him in a puzzled way. "You were out a long time," she said, as though not quite sure.

He had already decided what he would tell her. "Alice got away from me and I had to find her. I heard somebody's been setting traps back there in the woods, so I guess we'd better not take her there any more."

"I never do anyway," she said. "Go get yourself cleaned up, dinner's almost ready."

It took him a long time to feel warm again. He was glad she didn't notice the scratches on his hands from the briars. He wondered if he should warn her, but he didn't want to frighten her. They might go after her, just to get at him.

She had another headache that evening, and went to bed early. After she turned out the light, he went in and sat on the bed beside her.

"How do you know it isn't something serious?" he asked.

"I don't care if it is."

"Theresa, if something happened to you, I just couldn't deal with it."

"There's a lot I can't deal with, either," she said.

"I know. I won't try to rush you, but you can't stay like this forever."

"How do you expect me to stay?"

God, he couldn't handle any of this. Not her depression, his own depression, or Leonard firing shots at him. He was sure it had been Leonard. In the morning he would call the police and tell them about it, but there was still nothing he could prove.

He took Alice out for another walk, staying well inside the park, and finally went to bed.

He woke suddenly, hearing a crash and Alice barking. He sat up, his heart pounding. Theresa was up, too.

"It's somebody breaking in," she whispered.

He listened for a moment, and remembered the gunshots.

"It was glass," he said. "They can't get in through those awning windows."

"Don't go. It's dangerous. Pretend you're asleep."

Alice was still barking. Steady, even beats.

"I don't think anybody's inside," he said. "She wouldn't sound like that." He listened again, then cautiously made his way to the living room.

His foot touched glass. He groped on the shelf of the television table for a flashlight they kept there in case of power failure. When he shone it on the floor he saw a faint gleam of shattered glass and a dark, round shape. He bent to pick it up.

Theresa came down the hall behind him. "What is it?"

"A rock. Somebody threw a rock through the window."

She was silent for a moment. Then she said, "You should have left them alone."

"How do you know who it was?"

"I don't know. I only know—what he's like."

He heard the falter in her voice. As though wondering why she was saying it. But she didn't even know about the shooting.

Maybe the shots were only meant as a threat. He didn't think so. They had been too close.

156

He picked up the telephone.

"Who are you calling?" she asked.

"Nobody, I guess. It's dead. You want to bet the wires are cut?"

"Don't you dare go and look."

"Not now. I'll look in the morning."

"What are we going to do, Brian?"

"First," he said, "we're going to put plastic over the window. And then we're going to get a good night's sleep."

"How?"

He wasn't sure himself, but he knew that anything else would be counterproductive.

"I can't tell you how," he said, "but I can tell you why. Because that's what they don't want for us."

He couldn't be back. Not after she had thrown him out yesterday. And Leonard was still here, in the back bedroom, cleaning his gun. He would probably use it this time. Bonnie Ann, the stupid little brat, had mentioned Brian's visit, so she had had to tell Leonard what Brian was doing there, and she didn't think he believed her. He had practically accused her of having an affair.

Now Brian was back, but at least this time he didn't push his way in. He stood on the sun deck and asked politely, "May I use your phone for a minute?"

"Sure." She didn't feel very sure as she admitted him.

"Ours is out of order. I just want to report it."

"Sure. It's in there." He knew where it was. She motioned Bonnie to turn down the television. Bonnie stared at him curiously.

Cheryl went back to the sink where she had been washing the dishes, but she didn't turn on the water. She heard him dial. He gave his name and number. His phone wasn't working, he told them. Yes, completely dead. He had gone outside and it looked as though the wire had been cut. Yes, a clean cut. No, he had no idea, and that wasn't really the point. He only wanted it fixed.

She turned on the water and was scrubbing hardened egg yolk from a plate when he came back into the kitchen. She looked at him, not knowing what to say. If only he had mentioned to her that the wires had been cut. No reason why he should, but it would have been the logical thing to do. His silence on the subject made her uneasy.

"Thanks," he said.

"Oh. You're welcome." Stupidly she added, "I hope you get it fixed." She always talked too much when she was nervous.

"Today or tomorrow," he said. "I can't imagine who would do a thing like that. Cut our wires. Can you?"

After he left, she looked down at what she was doing and found herself washing a piece of leftover toast.

The window was no problem, he told Theresa. He could get that fixed through his work, and the phone would be taken care of right away.

"Are you going to tell the police?" she asked.

"Of course. I don't like being threatened this way. Why?"

"What are you going to tell them? That you think it was the Freaneys? Then you'll have to explain that you've been harassing them, and you'll have to tell them why."

"Harassing them?"

"Whatever you call it."

"Well, who do you think it was?" he asked.

"I don't know. But it could have been anybody."

"Why would it be?"

She didn't answer. Again he had the feeling that there was more going on than he knew. Something dangerous and frightening—and hers—and he didn't like not knowing what it was.

It was that voice, she thought. And the blackouts. They were all connected with her. It was like living on the edge of an invisible world that she couldn't hear, feel, or understand. Yet it caused things to happen that affected her life. And because she didn't know what went on in that world, she couldn't tell anyone about it. It might be something she didn't want them to know.

As Brian was leaving for work on Monday, he said, "Will you call me as soon as they fix the phone? I don't like you being left alone here without a phone."

"There are people all around," she pointed out.

"Yes, but—"

The Freaneys. He didn't trust Cheryl, and she was the closest. Most of the other nearby neighbors would be at work.

"I'm all right," she said, "and I'll call you."

"If I don't hear from you, I'll call the phone company. I'll keep after them," he promised.

After he left, she poured another cup of coffee. She had heard the voice again during the night. The voice that said it was Michael. She tried to recall whether she had ever known anyone named Michael. She thought it might be a memory that was trying to break through. Something that had a bearing on the present, perhaps.

She couldn't remember a Michael. But she had often had a feeling that there was someone else. Someone with her in the dark room.

Michael. He had said it as though she should recognize the name. But he did not seem surprised when she told him she didn't know him.

She wondered if he was there now. She set down her cup and asked softly, "Michael?"

She waited for almost a minute. Then she heard him.

"You're getting too close," he said.

She did not know whether it was a voice in her mind or in her ear. She thought it was her mind. And that meant he wasn't real.

"Too close to what?"

"The truth."

Something stabbed through her and made her afraid. The truth, he had said. Maybe she didn't want to know the truth.

"You might start to remember," the voice went on. "I don't want you to remember."

160

"I don't want to remember." She began to shiver.

"Sometimes in your sleep—"

"I don't want to remember."

"You won't be able to stop it if it comes. It's not a dream."

"Please go away."

"I can't go away. You won't let me."

"I want you to go. I don't want you here."

"If you want me to go," Michael told her, "there's something you have to do first. You have to die."

"I don't want you here."

"Are you willing to die? Never to wake up again?"

"No!"

She started up from her chair to turn on the radio. She wanted to drown him out. But she wanted to know who he was.

"Who are you?" she asked again. "And don't just tell me your name. Tell me who you are. Why are you here?"

"Ask yourself who you are," he replied.

"Stop that. I asked you a question."

"And I asked you a perfectly valid question."

This time she did turn on the radio. She would not listen to him any more. It wasn't even a him, it was a voice in her mind. She was crazy, hearing voices. Schizophrenic. Maybe it had happened long ago, in the dark room. Mrs. Sentry had driven her crazy.

Maybe the blackouts were part of it. And the times when she would suddenly find herself in a place that was unfamiliar, or doing something she couldn't explain. And the cigarettes. It was all her. No one else. She was crazy.

And afraid. She had no way of knowing what she might have done in those times when she wasn't there. When she had driven the car. She might have hurt somebody.

Hurt somebody . . .

She didn't know.

What if she had hurt somebody she loved?

161

21

Maynard Bundy wrote again about the killer:

"Psychiatrists tell us that most murderers harbor a conscious or unconscious desire to be caught." He cited the case of William Heirens, who scrawled in lipstick on a wall, "For heavens sake catch me before I kill more." "They elude the police," Bundy wrote, "but may leave secret clues or trails as a hidden cry for help. Many a deranged killer in the grip of some uncontrollable rage is unable to stop himself, but afterward feels a terrible guilt. He cries out for external control. To be stopped.

"The key word is guilt," continued the columnist. "A sociopathic killer, on the other hand, lacks the mechanism for feeling guilt or remorse. He has no desire to be caught and punished. He may want the recognition and fame his crimes will bring him, but the risks of capture are too great. He knows his deeds are famous, and that will have to suffice. In his fantasies he has achieved the redress he sought. He has terrorized the public, and that satisfies him. Since the cyanide killer leaves no clues or other signs that point to him as an individual, police theorize that he is probably sociopathic. The remote and random nature of his crimes seems to bear this out. Without a single clue to follow, the police may find it almost impossible to track him down."

"Almost impossible," Brian raged. "Why doesn't he just say it's impossible, and pin another medal on the guy?"

It was evening. Brian had waited all day for a chance to look at the newspaper. After dinner, he had pushed aside the dishes and spread it out on the table. He read the news first. Then Bundy. He already knew Boyd Wentz had been cleared. Jess Morehouse assured him that they were still following up on Wentz's connections.

"I think Bundy did it himself," he said as Theresa began to clear the table. "Talk about sense of fame. He can be his own publicist. Wait, I'll help you with those. I just want to finish the paper."

"It's okay," she said. "You work all day and I don't."

"Do I dare ask what you did with your day?"

She gave him a quick look and went back to stacking the plates. "Just piddled it away, I guess."

"Doing what?"

"That's what housework is."

"Housework all day in this small place?"

"Not all day. Sometimes I sit and think."

"That's what you shouldn't do."

"I'm not going to forget her, Brian."

"It's not just that, is it?" he said.

"What do you mean?"

From the way she looked at him, he knew he had hit something.

"I don't know exactly what I mean, but I get the feeling it's more than Patty. Sometimes you act as if you're scared of something."

This time he knew he had reached her. She tried to look at him and couldn't. She hurried to the kitchen and dropped her dishes with a crash onto the counter.

"Anything break?" he asked.

"No." Then she said, "I was carrying too much."

He could have been merciless. He wanted to shake her out of this, but he didn't want to hurt her.

163

"Maybe I could take some vacation time," he said. "Maybe we could go somewhere."

She turned and looked at him, hopefully. "Could we?"

"Would you like that?"

"I'd love to get away. But where?"

"I don't know. It'd be nice if we had the money for Florida. Someplace different. Would you like Florida?"

"I don't know if I'd like anything, but I want to get away."

"I'll work on it," he promised.

He returned to the paper while she washed the dishes. He read again what Bundy had written about sociopathic killers. And he knew there was more to it than simply catching the man. Or woman. He knew they had to build up a case. If catching him would be hard without clues, building up the case would be that much harder.

The thing to do was identify him. That was the first thing. Find him and then somehow make him confess. Bully him. If Brian could think of an airtight way, and then take it to the police . . .

He would be on thin ice. Very thin. A person could always retract a confession, even one given to the police. He would have to seal it completely. He didn't know how. He didn't know the rules. But before that, he would have to find the killer.

He watched Theresa slowly sponging the dishes. She seemed lost somewhere, deep in thought.

"Theresa," he said, "how do you see the rest of your life?"

She stopped moving.

"I don't," she answered.

It worried him. "You mean you just don't think about it?"

"I don't see what there is."

"Do you realize that I'm still here?"

"Yes, I know." He could hear the guilt in her voice. He wondered what it would be like never to feel guilty.

"You haven't lost everything," he said. "Maybe the most important thing."

She put the dish towel to her face and began to cry.

164

"I'm sorry, I shouldn't have said that." He pushed back his chair and went to her. He had pulled her close to him before he remembered that she didn't like to be touched. "I shouldn't have said it. Here I was, thinking about guilt, and I'm trying to give you a guilt trip."

After a minute or two, she managed to control herself. "Thinking about—?"

"Guilt. How this guy doesn't feel guilty, so he doesn't want to be caught. That's what it says in the paper."

She walked away as though she had forgotten him, and sat down to look at the paper.

"It's in Bundy's column," he told her.

She turned to the editorial page.

"Don't you ever read the paper any more?" he asked. It had been there all day. She didn't answer. Even when she finished reading, she sat looking thoughtful.

"What do you make of it?" he asked. "Do we know anybody like that?"

She seemed not to hear him. He had never seen her like that before, tuning him out so completely.

He thought about Leonard. Did the description fit Leonard? He certainly didn't seem to feel much guilt about the way he treated his wife and kids. Maybe because he didn't really beat them. Not regularly, anyway. A lot of men who beat their families were sorry afterward. With Leonard, it was a more insidious kind of thing. Lou Fiedler had called it psychological abuse. It was something Leonard did all the time, not only when he was drunk. It only got worse when he was drunk, and even then he wasn't sorry afterward.

Was he ever sorry?

But was he creative enough to pull off this cyanide thing?

Brian slid the paper away from her and folded it. Alice came over to him. He patted her head. "In a little while, girl. We'll have a nice walk." He said to Theresa, "You know, it's damn lucky we have this dog, not only for companionship, but she makes a good excuse to hang around outside."

He hadn't thought she was listening. But after a moment,

165

she said, "Brian, why don't you leave those people alone?"

"Why? You never give me a really good reason."

"Because you might get into trouble."

She didn't know about the shooting. She did know about the rock and the telephone wire, and maybe it had frightened her the way it was meant to. He refused to be terrorized.

"What trouble?" he asked.

She seemed vague but disturbed. "Something might happen."

"Something's already happened," he said. "That's the whole point."

He watched her turn and go toward the bedroom, her fist pressed to her mouth. She knows something, he thought again. But he wasn't sure that even she knew what it was.

22

Cheryl waited until they were in bed before she told him. He was apt to be mellower then, and not inclined to blame everything on her.

"Sweetie?" She traced his jawline with her fingers. "I'm scared."

He raised himself up on his elbow. "You're scared, kitten? What are you scared of?"

She tried not to whimper or whine. "Something's happening and I don't know what it is."

"What are you talking about?"

"Well—it's Brian. And it's not what you think, it's what I said before. He's still—"

"Huh?" He pressed down on her, crushing her.

"I told you, it's not that. It's not—He keeps watching me. Us," she added hastily. "I guess it's all of us. He acts as if we did something wrong."

"What are you talking about?"

"Because of Patty. I think he's suspicious."

"What's he got to be suspicious about?"

"I don't know. I just know he keeps watching. He asks questions. He keeps—" Her voice grew tighter. She rolled her head back and forth, frustrated at her inadequate explanation. "He keeps bugging me. I want him to stop."

"He comes over here?"

Oh, Lord, he was getting the wrong idea again.

"He keeps bugging me about the poison. He asks questions."

"Do you let him in?"

"Not any more." He hadn't been in the house for a day or two. She had never thought of keeping him out. She just couldn't be rude to a man whose daughter had died in her home.

"Does he try anything?"

"I'm not talking about that. It's nothing like that. It's the way he watches us. It's as if he's trying to trap us. He thinks we killed Patty."

"Huh?"

"I'm sure that's what he thinks. Because the poison was here."

"That's what he thinks, huh?"

"I know it is."

"The guy's nuts."

An odd chill pricked at her nerves. She refused to explore it. She only thought: It couldn't have been anybody here. It's our own house.

"I guess so," she said. "A thing like that can make a person sort of crazy."

"What did you tell him?"

"Nothing. What's to tell?" She was glad she could say that.

Leonard lay back and stared up at the ceiling. "You know what I think? I think it's her."

"What do you mean? Who?"

"Theresa."

"I don't know what you mean. What did she do?"

"I think she planted that stuff."

"Planted the poison? You must be out of your mind. It was her own kid."

"She never meant her own kid to get it."

"*Theresa?* You're out of your mind."

"Do you think Theresa's playing with a full deck?"

"Well, no. But like I said, a thing like that can make a person crazy. I'd go crazy."

"You would, huh?"

"Sure I would."

"Especially if you knew you did it."

"Oh, Leonard, knock it off. What would she do it for?"

"I told you, she never meant it for her own kid. She meant it for us. Probably me."

"What the hell ever for?"

"Something that happened a while back. You know, Theresa and me both grew up in this town."

"Yes, but she's much younger than you. She never talked about you. It's like she didn't even know you."

"I guess she didn't. We weren't even in the same part of town."

"It's not that big a place," Cheryl said. "You mean you knew Theresa? Why didn't you ever tell me?"

"Will you shut up and let me talk? It was back one summer—I can't remember. The early sixties, maybe. I was over to see this kid I knew. Bobby Durks. There was a bunch of guys. About four guys."

She ran the dates through her mind. He was thirty-nine now. He must have been in high school at the time he was talking about.

"These four guys," he said, "we hung around together. Bobby lived on Creighton Avenue, where there was this old house. It's torn down now. The old lady had a little kid living there."

"You mean Theresa? Why didn't you ever tell me?"

"Will you shut up and listen?"

"But Theresa never said anything!"

"Shut up, will you? Anyhow, these guys—It wasn't me, don't get me wrong, I had nothing to do with it. The three of them had a little too much beer one time. They got hold of this kid—"

169

"Theresa?"

"That's who I'm talking about, stupid. They got hold of her and, you know, they did what guys do sometimes when they have too much beer."

"You mean they raped her? My God! How old was she?"

"How the hell do I know?"

"But—" Theresa was twenty-nine. Ten years younger than Leonard. If he was in high school—"She must have been just a little kid."

"That's what I said. I don't know. Seven, eight."

"But how come she never—You two never—"

"I told you, I wasn't involved. Maybe she forgot. But that's why I never said anything."

"How could she forget a thing like that?"

"Who the hell knows? But she sure never acted like she remembered. Anyhow, that's not all. I guess she must have gone and told that lady she lived with. I guess the lady didn't believe her, because she went and told me this kid was spreading dirty lies about us."

"Why didn't you tell her it was true?"

"God, are you stupid or something? So the guys got hold of her again and they knocked her around a little. They were going to teach her a lesson."

"For what?"

"For snitching."

"Dear God! Why didn't you stop them?"

"Will you shut up? I'm talking. How do you stop people? I wasn't even there. They told me about it. They took her out to this place down the road, a sand quarry. Few miles down. It's not there any more. They dug a hole and said they were going to bury her. They just wanted to give her a little scare. Nothing serious. So they put her in like it was a grave and got her all covered; then they were going to dig her out. But the sand was dry and it kept sliding back in. There we were digging with our hands like a bunch of idiots and the sand kept sliding

170

back in. I remember I got scared she was really going to die, and somebody might have seen her with us. Oh, shit. By the time we got her out she was half dead and we were really pissed off."

Cheryl waited. At first he had said he wasn't there. She wanted him not to have been there.

She managed to whisper, "What happened then?"

"So they knocked her around for giving us a scare. Then we went home. Bobby had a jeep. He wouldn't take her with us. We left her there. I guess she must have walked all the way home, because she showed up later."

Cheryl felt cold. This is what it's like, she thought. This is what it's like when it's over.

She moaned, "Oh, sweetie," but her mouth felt as though it were strapped shut.

"I told you it wasn't me," he said. "I had nothing to do with it. I guess she didn't remember what happened, but maybe now she's starting to remember. I'm the one who's still here, so maybe she tried to take it out on me. You know how it is with crazy people."

She didn't trust herself to speak. Her silence seemed to make him nervous.

"You see what I mean?" he said. "Maybe that's what happened with the sugar. She's trying to get back at me."

Poor Theresa, thought Cheryl. She never had a chance in her whole life.

But if Theresa was the one who left that poison—Why, it could have hit any one of them. Cheryl never did anything to her, and neither did the children.

He ran his hand over her thigh. "How about a little action?"

She rolled away from him.

"What the hell's this?" he demanded.

"I just can't right now."

"What do you mean you can't? You had your period last week. You should be in top form."

"You don't understand."

"The hell I don't. I told you I had nothing to do with what happened." He ripped off her nightgown.

She curled into a tight ball. "Oh, go to hell. Go have a beer."

"Yeah?"

She could feel him looming over her. She cringed when the blow came. She had expected it. Then the bed heaved again as he got out of it. She heard him rustling around, and then his tread in the hallway. He really was going for a beer. She had gotten off more easily than she had expected.

The footsteps stopped. She heard a door bang open, and his voice, roaring. She jumped out of bed and ran into the hall. It was Mark's room. He had the light on. She sagged against the wall. Why couldn't the little shit ever learn to obey his father? No reading in bed. It would save so much trouble.

She didn't even need the sound effects to know what was happening. She rushed back to bed, curled into a ball again, and clamped the pillow over her head.

Brian thought he was getting close when he heard the uproar. They were starting to break, he thought.

He was out at seven-thirty the next morning, checking the oil in his car, when the children left for school. They left separately. Mark was first. There was never much closeness between those two. Four years' difference in age, for one thing.

Neither child spoke to him. Mark didn't even look at him as he walked past and on up the road to the bus stop. Brian went back inside and waited until Leonard left for work. He telephoned Reynolds to tell them he would be a little late. Couldn't get his car started, he said. And then he went over and knocked on Cheryl's door.

He heard her gasp when she opened it. She stared at him and couldn't seem to think of anything to say.

"Everything all right?" he asked.

172

She pressed her lips together and looked away. He had to squeeze past her to get into the kitchen.

"It's none of my business," he said, "but I heard a lot of yelling last night, and I know how things are, so I just wanted to be sure everything's okay."

"It's all right," she said, still not looking at him. And it wasn't any of his business. Not the part he knew about. The yelling, as he called it. That was her fault. It wouldn't have been so bad if she had been willing to make love to Leonard. She should have forced herself. He had caught her by surprise right after telling her that horrible thing, and she knew he had been in the middle of it, even though he said he wasn't.

She wondered how much Theresa remembered.

"How come you're not at work?" she asked.

"As I said, I just wanted to be sure everything was all right. I thought you might need a friend."

"A what?" Him?

"Somebody was in pain," he said. "Or scared."

"It's okay. It's just—It's okay."

He stood close to her, his arms folded. What was he looking for, bruises?

Or maybe this was what they meant by "leaning on." He wasn't touching her, but he was leaning on her, putting pressure on. In another minute she was going to fly all to pieces.

She wished she could just disappear. Go somewhere else, far away from all this. Be somebody else. Get away from Brian, from her own family. Or maybe she would take Bonnie with her.

"You know what I mean," he said. "I'll see you, Cheryl."

After the door closed behind him, she went into the living room and sat down. From there, she could see his house. What was better, she could have peace. It was all she wanted. Peace. She couldn't take any more of this.

She wondered if she could ever face Leonard again. Really face him. Make love with him.

173

"No," she whimpered, curling into a ball. She couldn't even stand to have him touch her.

Poor Theresa. She imagined it happening to Bonnie. How could they have done it?

Teenage boys could get carried away. But that? Not one bit of compassion. No decency. She had been just Bonnie's age. In Cheryl's mind, Theresa and Bonnie became mixed up. Over and over again she saw it happening to Bonnie. The rape, the blows, the burial in the sand pit. And no one to protect her. No one to believe her story, or care.

How would she face him? He had still been angry at breakfast and hadn't talked much, but how would she face him for the whole rest of her life?

Brian thought of taking the day off. He was late anyway, but he couldn't keep doing this. He would be out of a job and then they'd have worse trouble.

Maybe he was wrong, the way he kept being drawn to the Freaneys. He could have been wrong. He had a feeling about it, and he tried to figure out where the feeling came from.

He arrived at work half an hour late, glad that he didn't have to punch a time clock. They expected him to be responsible, and he had failed. He sold a bathtub enclosure and a rooftop exhaust fan without knowing what he was doing. The roof fans were on sale and he forgot to charge the sale price. The customer corrected him.

He decided he would go home for lunch. He told Joe Williams he would be a little longer than usual.

"If you don't feel good," said Joe, "maybe you oughtta stay home."

"No, that's okay." He hadn't thought in terms of being sick, but he supposed that was what it looked like to other people. "I can't take too much time off. My wife and I are planning a vacation."

He called first to be sure Theresa was there. He needed her to be there. She sounded surprised that he was coming home.

174

"Is tuna fish okay?" she asked. "Tuna sandwich?"

His lunch was ready when he arrived. He was grateful for her efficiency. It would help get him back to work in some kind of time.

"Listen," he said as she poured him a cup of coffee, "do you mind if we talk about Patty?"

Her lips parted and she looked at him warily. "Why?"

"I've been thinking. I screwed up at work today, thinking about that sugar."

She sat down heavily. He guessed she didn't want to talk about the sugar, but she didn't say anything.

"If Patty saw a box of sugar in somebody else's house," he began, "even the Freaneys' house, and it wasn't opened yet. Sealed shut. And she wanted some. Say she wanted to sweeten some candy, the way the police think. Do you think she'd open a box that the Freaneys hadn't opened yet?"

Theresa looked at him. Across her face, the skin seemed to tighten. Her dark eyes stared. He found himself breathing a little faster, wondering what it was all about.

"No," she said. "Not Patty."

"You're sure?"

Her fingers worked at the handle of her coffee cup. She was trying to get hold of it.

"Not Patty."

"That's what I thought."

She did not ask him what he meant. Maybe she was ahead of him on that.

He said, "Don't get sore. I want to go over and see Cheryl for a minute." He knew she was home. Her car was there. He finished his lunch and then went over to Cheryl's house.

She must not have noticed him approaching. She came to the door and he saw her shocked face through the narrow pane. He held up a finger. One more question. He didn't know whether she got the message, but she opened the door.

"Just a moment of your time," he said. He wondered how he had gotten so hardened to talking about Patty's death.

175

"What do you want?"

"I want to know something. One thing, about that sugar. Did you open the box after you got it home?"

She blinked. "Why?"

"I want to know if you opened the box."

"No." Her voice came out with a rising inflection, like a question.

"What did you do with if after you brought it home?"

"I put it away."

"Where?"

"In the—" She stopped. She was heading into quicksand and she knew it.

"*In* the," he exclaimed triumphantly. "Not *on* the. You put it away, you said. In the cupboard? Theresa keeps things like that in a cupboard. Until she opens them, and then she puts them in a canister. So it wasn't opened."

She made no reply.

"Thanks, Cheryl." He turned from the door and went home.

Theresa was sitting at the table where he had left her.

"Cheryl says the box wasn't opened," he told her. "Said she put it away after she brought it home. In something. Probably a cupboard. And we agree that Patty wouldn't have gotten it out or opened it by herself. So it must have been opened and in plain sight. What does that tell you?"

The victorious tone in his voice was lost on her. She huddled over and bowed her head.

"What's the matter?" he asked.

"Nothing. I'm okay."

"The hell you are. You look cold. Why don't you put on a heavier sweater? Or push up the thermostat?"

"I'm okay, Brian."

"You sure?"

She didn't answer. He said, "I have to get back to work. You'd better be okay by the time I come home tonight."

"Goodbye." She got up from the table and put her arms

around him. She held him tightly, as if she was afraid to have him leave.

"Hey," he said, "it's only a couple of hours. Three or four hours. Do you want me to stay?"

"No. It's all right."

"You sure?"

"I'm sure. Goodbye." She gave him a long kiss. She didn't want it to end any more than he did. Maybe he should have taken the afternoon off.

The kiss had dazzled him. Only on his way back to work did he think about what she had said. "Goodbye." Not just "'Bye," or "See you." She acted as though he were going away for a long time. Or as if she was.

He almost turned back, but decided he was overreacting, and drove on into the village.

23

She wondered where he was now.

"I hate you," she said into the empty room. There was no answer.

Why? Why had he done it?

She didn't know anything that went on in his mind. And yet he seemed to know her mind. He knew all about her, even her past. Because, probably, he had been there and she hadn't.

"Why did you do it?" she asked. "Didn't you know what might happen?"

He couldn't have known. How could anyone know? She wondered if he even cared. What was Patty to him?

"But you're me," she said. "Aren't you? Doesn't Patty mean anything to you?"

Again there was silence. But she didn't need an answer. She knew it. He was not the same as Theresa. He was Michael. He was altogether different. If he shared her body—Theresa's body, a woman's body—he was still Michael.

"I hate you for what you did. I hate you." Tears came into her eyes. She put a hand to her head where the pain was beginning. She knew it now. He was trying to get out.

"Not this time," she told him. "And never again. Never again." She got up from her chair, stiff and bent like an old woman. Tears streamed down her face.

"You killed her. You made me kill her. My own little girl."

She went to the kitchen and looked out at her car, parked in the driveway below the window. If she used her car, someone would see her. Unless she took it to a remote place. But that would be too long. She had to do it quickly, before he came out.

She could take her car and drive over a cliff. But she didn't want it to hurt. And it had to be now.

She looked around the kitchen. There were knives. She couldn't stab herself, even knowing it was Michael.

The oven. It would be painless. She opened the door and crouched down to see inside. She took out the shelf and put it on top of the sink. Her headache was pounding. The gas might make it worse. Would he be able to come out then?

Her next obstacle was the pilot light. If she could reach back there to blow it out . . . She would have to take out the bottom shelf. She stacked it with the other. And she blew. The pilot light flickered. She took another breath. It went out. She reached up to turn on the gas.

Brian was worried. What did she mean with that "good-bye"?

Joe Williams came toward him, pulling in his stomach to make himself look emaciated. "Tomorrow," he said, "it's my turn to eat lunch."

"Sorry," Brian told him. "I didn't mean to take so long. I'm worried about my wife." He was seized by a customer who wanted to order storm windows.

"We'll have to send somebody out to measure—" Brian began.

"I've got the measurements right here." The customer pulled a crumpled piece of paper from his pocket. Brian hated this. They insisted they had measured, and half the time they'd done it wrong. Then they blamed the store when the windows didn't fit.

He'd call her later. When this crowd cleared out. If she

didn't answer, he'd call a neighbor to check on her. Even Cheryl, if she didn't hang up on him. With a stump of a pencil, he wrote down the measurements. Twenty-one and seven-sixteenths of an inch. God.

She gagged on the smell. They added the smell on purpose so people couldn't poison themselves by mistake. They should have a way of taking it out. An option, like the pilot light.

"Brian!"
It was Dorian. He couldn't see her now without thinking of Cliff.
"Can I help you with anything?" he asked.
"I want to see the attic fans. I also want to see you." She fluttered her lashes.
"Anything wrong?" He felt as though he had been asking that all day.
"No. I just wondered if you'd like to stop over after work. Cliffie's been doing this big project for science, and it's absolutely brilliant."
"I have to get home," he said. "I'm worried about Theresa."
"Why, is she sick?"
"She just seemed upset. It was something she said. I'm worried."
"Why don't you give her a call?"
"I've been trying to. This place is a mob scene, with the sale."
"Call her and see if she's okay, and then plan on coming over. Just for a little while. It would mean so much. He really needs a man in his life."
"You didn't tell him, did you?"
"Brian, you already asked me that. Of course I didn't. All he knows is that you're important to him. Please?"
"I'll call her and let you know."
"Do that. Now can we look at the fans?"

180

He had to explain the fans in detail. She wanted to know how they worked, what she needed to do about them, how often they required lubricating. Finally he left her to make up her mind. He was heading toward the pay phone when a customer accosted him. He took care of the customer, and then Dorian was back. She had made her decision. He wrote up the sale. She asked him when she could expect him.

"I haven't reached Theresa yet," he said.

"Maybe she's out shopping."

"No, I mean I haven't had a chance to call her."

"Don't you get a coffee break or anything? Look, I have to get back to the store. I'm off early today. Four o'clock."

"I'll let you know."

An hour later he managed to get to a telephone. It rang six times before Theresa answered.

"You okay?" he asked.

"Why not?"

"I just wondered. You sound out of breath. I might be late tonight. About an hour. You don't mind, do you?"

"Why should I?" she asked.

"Okay, I'll see you then. Take care."

He felt dazed. She had certainly changed from the way she was at his noontime visit. But her voice sounded odd. In any case, he would be able to get Dorian off his back. He didn't know how he felt about Cliff. He didn't want to get attached. But maybe he already was.

After hanging up the telephone, Michael went to the bathroom and splashed his face with cold water. He felt like hell. The bitch had tried to kill him. He almost hadn't gotten out in time.

He dried his face. Maybe he should put his whole head under the shower. It felt as though it was full of sharp rocks. He needed his faculties to stay in control.

She would try again. He turned on the shower and drenched himself. It was cold, but it didn't help clear his

181

head. He was only half there. She would take over again and kill them both.

"You've got to stay dead, Theresa," he said aloud, hoping she would hear him, but knowing she wouldn't listen. "Stay dead. Stay dead. . . ."

Cliff had done a project with magnets and magnetic fields. He had drawn diagrams that looked like something out of a textbook.

Brian turned to Dorian. "Did we know stuff like this in the fifth grade?"

"I don't know stuff like this even now," she laughed, clearly enjoying her "family." "How about another beer?"

"No, thanks. I have to get home. This is really impressive, Cliff."

The boy tried to be modest about it, but a grin broke through. Brian was glad he looked like his mother, even to the aquamarine eyes. He thought the kid might have more brains than both of them together.

He looked at his watch. He had stayed an hour and a half.

"God, I told my wife an hour."

"She doesn't time you, does she?" Dorian asked. "Why don't you give her another call?"

"And tell her what?" He remembered how Theresa had sounded when he phoned that afternoon. He couldn't remember her exact words, but she didn't seem to give a damn that he was going to be late.

"Tell her you're staying for dinner," Dorian said.

"I can't do that."

"Why not? I have sliced beef from the store. We can make sandwiches and cole slaw. You used to like that."

She had built a fire in the fireplace. Her home was warm and pleasant with happiness and friendliness. And Cliff was his son. He should spend more time with his son.

"Go on. Call." She picked up the telephone. He took it from her and dialed his number.

"There's no answer," he said, as the empty ringing went on and on.

"What are you worried about, exactly?"

"I don't know. I'm just worried."

"For heaven's sake, Brian, she's probably out visiting one of her friends.

"You don't understand. Theresa doesn't have friends."

"You mean there's nobody in that whole park she might drop in on?"

"Maybe, but not since Patty died. She hasn't bothered with anybody since then."

"Did it ever occur to you that she might start feeling better someday?"

Again he remembered how she had sounded earlier. Maybe Dorian was right. Maybe it was wrong of him to keep worrying about her.

He glanced at his watch again, but didn't really note the time. "I'll try again in a little while," he said.

"Good. We'll start the cole slaw right now."

It wasn't Michael who had pulled her away from the oven, it was Alice. Or maybe Alice had somehow called Michael out. To save her. But Alice didn't understand.

"It's not fair to you, is it?" she said, stroking the golden neck. "It's not fair to lose Patty and then me, but he's got to die for what he did, Alice, because I can't live with it. And you can't interfere. Come on, girl."

She took Alice's collar and led her outside. Her car was still warm from the day's sunshine, even though the sun was long gone. She shut Alice inside it, opening one of the windows a few inches for air. Then she went back to the house.

He would be home soon. He had said an hour, and it was

past that now. She would have to hurry. And hurry before Michael could come back. She needed something quicker. The belt from his bathrobe, or Alice's leash. It would be unpleasant, perhaps even painful. But quick.

Cliff said, "Mom, a car just came. It's Mr. Aiken."

"Oh, hell," said Dorian, not loudly. She didn't want Cliff to hear.

"Shall I let him in?"

"We can't not let him in."

"Maybe I'd better go," said Brian.

"No, don't," Dorian told him. "He doesn't own me, and he should know it."

"I'd rather not be the one to tell him. In fact, I'd rather not be here at all when Aiken comes in."

But it was too late to escape, and besides, Aiken would have seen his car. Brian grabbed his jacket and was putting it on when the doorbell rang.

"We're almost ready to eat," Dorian said as Cliff went to answer it.

"I'm sure Henry would love a home-cooked meal. Sorry, Dorian. Some other time."

He passed Henry in the doorway. "Hello, there. Came to measure for storm windows. Have a nice evening, folks."

Dorian and Cliff waved goodbye from the picture window. He hoped Henry wouldn't be too hard on her. She was quite right that he didn't own her, but you couldn't tell that to a person like Henry.

He felt a little foggy from the beer. One beer, but it had been on an empty stomach. He began to wish he hadn't had it. Theresa would smell it on him and think he had been carousing. And to her mind, he probably had.

He was surprised to find Alice in Theresa's car when he reached home. The door was unlocked. He opened it and the dog jumped out with a wild greeting.

The house was dark, but he could see Theresa in the

184

kitchen. Grasping Alice's collar, he hurried around to the door.

Theresa was still in the kitchen, leaning against the sink when she went inside.

"Did you know you forgot your dog in the car?" he said. "And what are you doing with all the lights off?"

And then he waited, prepared for anything. It was quite possible that she had broken down completely.

She stared at him as though she hadn't expected him at all. As though he didn't belong there.

"You okay?" he asked.

"I'm fine. Why?"

"You seemed pretty upset when I left this afternoon. That's why I called."

"You did? What's the matter, don't you think I can take care of myself?"

Belligerent again. She wasn't usually like that. "Anything wrong?"

Her hand was pressed to the side of her head.

"Another headache?" he asked.

"Mind your own damn business."

"Huh?"

"You heard me."

"You sound like Cheryl."

"The hell I do. I sound like myself. It's that goddamned—" She walked heavily down the hall to the bathroom. He heard water running. Taking something for her headache. At least she didn't seem depressed any more. Just angry. Unbelievably angry. He had never heard her talk like that before.

At the end of the hall, he saw her go into the bedroom. He heard one of the closet doors slide open. The she reappeared, wearing a jacket of his.

"Going out?" he asked in surprise.

She stopped for a moment and looked at him. A confused, hostile stare.

He reached out a hand, but that was as far as he took it. He didn't dare try to touch her when she was like that.

185

"What's gotten into you?" he asked.

"What do you mean?" Her voice was low. At least he had finally made contact with her.

"I mean, you're different. You're not like you."

"So?"

He had lost the contact.

"Is that so bad?" she went on. "Not being me? I'm getting out of here."

"Getting out?"

"I'm leaving. I don't belong here. You must have figured that out."

"I don't know what you're talking about." He seized her arm. She twisted out of his grasp and punched him away with a blow that hurt his shoulder. Before he could react, she put her hand to her head again. She stood for a moment as though frozen, her eyes glassy. Then she blinked rapidly and gave a little whimper.

"Brian," she said.

"Who did you think it was?" The question was almost a play for time. Something was wrong here. He couldn't understand it.

"You were talking funny," he told her.

She whispered, "Michael." Whoever the hell that was. Then she ran her fingers over her throat. "Your belt."

"My belt?"

"He—"

She never finished. She put her hands over her face.

"I'm still going to kill him!" she screamed. "And kill myself!"

He grabbed her by the shoulders. "Theresa!"

"I'm going to kill him! And kill myself!"

"No, honey, I know we—I talked about—But that's not the way. And we can't prove anything." He took her arm again and tried to calm her.

"Sweetheart, I know you're upset. I am, too, but we can't live like this. We can make a life for ourselves. We'll tell the police what we know, what we found out today, and we'll let

186

them take care of it." He was leading her toward the bedroom. "I want you to rest for a while. I'm going to call the doctor and see if he can give you something to make you feel better."

"No, you don't understand." She was crying now. "It's him."

He was afraid of her. She was totally irrational. He would have to get the doctor quickly before she did something terrible. What if he was wrong about the Freaneys?

"You just rest, honey. Take it easy." He helped her onto the bed, then went to get a washcloth which he dampened with hot water. He placed it on her forehead. "This'll help you feel better. I'll be back in a minute." He was sure she could sense his hurry. He couldn't help it. "I'll be back in a minute," he said again, and went down the hall to the telephone.

He had barely finished dialing when he heard the back door open and close.

He dropped the phone. Good God, she was outside. And murderous.

He flung open the front door. He stood on the steps, looking through the darkness. There were lights in the houses all around him. A television picture danced in the next trailer. He saw the trees, and a clothesline in back with laundry still on it, but he couldn't see her.

He took a breath to call her, and let it out slowly. She would never answer. He went back inside and grabbed the jacket he had thrown over a chair. He slipped on Alice's leash and took her out with him.

He circled the back, where the storage shed and the fuel tanks were. He coaxed Alice, but the dog hadn't picked up a trail, or didn't know what to do with it. Theresa wouldn't be there anyway. She had a purpose.

Thank God Leonard wasn't home yet. At least his car wasn't there. He walked around the Freaneys' trailer, but he didn't find her outside. He thought he would know if she had gone in, but he knocked on the door.

It was opened by Bonnie.

"Is my wife here?" he asked.

They all looked at him, Cheryl and the two kids.

"I have to find her. I think she's sick." Still they didn't move. He blurted, "She said she was going to kill him."

Cheryl clapped her hand to her mouth. She knew something. He couldn't think about that now.

"It's because of the sugar," Brian said. "You have to understand, she's crazy with grief." It sounded phony, but it was true. "I have to find her before she does something."

Mark was wearing the shirt he had worn that night his father locked him out. The navy blue shirt with Scalzo Motors on the back. The kind they wore in the service division.

The service division. Boyd Wentz. The kids knew Boyd Wentz.

He forgot everything. Theresa. Everything. He had been right. The Freaneys. Now he knew.

He felt as though time and space had come to an end. There was only Mark's face. A marble mask. And he knew.

24

Leonard turned off the highway into the trailer park. He'd needed that drink before coming home. He could have kicked his butt all the way to Pennsylvania for telling Cheryl about that thing with Theresa. It made sense as a way of explaining why Theresa had it in for him, but he wished like hell that he hadn't told Cheryl. He might have known she'd get on her high horse.

His lights caught a figure in the middle of the road. Damn jerk. He was about to blow his horn when he saw who it was.

Holy shit, the bitch just stood there holding out her arms, blocking his way. This wasn't for real. And that expression on her face. He couldn't believe it was Theresa.

She started toward him. He shouldn't have had that drink. He couldn't make his mind work, and his guts were turning to water. He took his foot off the brake and put it on the gas pedal. He twisted the wheel. She would have to get out of the way.

She hit the car like a bomb, flinging herself across the hood. He let out a yell. The car went up an embankment onto somebody's lawn. A light burst in front of his face as she punched her fist through the windshield.

He yelled again. With a hand like that, she could smash him to pieces. Theresa?

He couldn't get across the seat to the far side. Damned hump in the middle. He pushed open the door and tried to run. She was on him, pummeling blows with the strength of a man. He flailed at her but couldn't catch her. He could only shield his face.

Somewhere he heard a scream. She let up for only a second, long enough for him to scramble to his feet. He couldn't get to his car, couldn't get home. She would be all over him. He lit out for the woods at the side of the road. Wasn't thinking. He only wanted to hide in the dark.

He couldn't see his way through the underbrush. He tripped and she was on top of him. His head cracked against something hard. More lights flashed. He flung out his arm like a blinded bull and felt it connect with something soft.

"They went in the woods!" Cheryl screamed. She stood freezing in her sweatshirt in the middle of the road.

People were popping out of houses. Leonard's car still sat halfway up on the grass, its engine running. The door was open. There was a hole in the windshield where it must have hit something, or Leonard's head had gone through.

Brian ran toward the woods. They were out there somewhere but he couldn't see or hear them. He had to find her. She had broken down completely and the bastard would kill her. He couldn't waste precious time going back for a flashlight.

"Go, girl," he told Alice. "You can find her."

He saw Cheryl running toward her house as he got into Leonard's car. He turned it around to face the woods. The tree trunks shone whitely in the reflected light. He couldn't see beyond them.

In a daze, Mark watched his mother dial the telephone. They knew. He couldn't think what to do. It was all too sudden, too fast.

190

"Police?" she shrieked. "Something's happening! My husband—they're trying to kill him!" She drew in a heavy, quivering breath.

"Freaney," she said, more calmly. "Winding Creek Trailer Park, Number Forty-six, third row. They've gone in the woods. She's trying to kill him."

She hung up the phone. Her hair was disheveled, her eyes smudged.

Then she noticed the children. "You two kids just go to your rooms," she snapped. "Go and stay there. I don't know what might happen."

They turned and scurried down the hall. Bonnie wanted to talk to him, but he closed himself in his room. He couldn't think. He should be getting out of here, but where? His mother had meant to protect them, not knowing how he would be when he came back. Like a crazy man. He would come raging in—and it shouldn't even be happening. He should have been long dead.

And now Patty's father knew.

Bewildered, Theresa clung to a tree. She could hear someone, or something, crashing nearby. She hugged the tree and tried not to breathe. Her heart was pounding. It would give her away.

Brian? She had trusted him. Then he had started calling the doctor and she ran away. It was all she remembered.

But this wasn't Brian. It was something that threatened her life. Somehow she knew.

She only wished she had some idea of why she was there.

The crashing came closer. She heard the thing wheeze heavily. It was down on the ground, feeling among the leaves.

"Crazy bitch," it muttered.

Leonard Freaney. A cold terror washed over her. Leonard . . . Len, they called him. Something had happened, long ago. She couldn't remember. It was happening now. There

191

were hands all over her, holding her down. Terrible pain. And then the sand. Sand in her nose and mouth. Her dream—

"You're a hell of a dog," Brian said. He thought all dogs could pick up a trail. He stumbled out to the road into a crowd of people. Cheryl ran toward him.

"I couldn't find them," he said.

She was breathing hard. "I called the police." He didn't know whether that was good or bad. He didn't know what was happening, but in the distance he heard a siren.

Cheryl had put on a coat. She pulled a crumpled green kerchief out of her pocket and blotted her tears. "I guess he had it coming," she sobbed. "It was so horrible."

"You knew about it?"

The siren came closer. It was on the last hill approaching the park.

"He only told me last night," she said. "He thought that was why Theresa wanted to kill him. He didn't think she remembered. She never said anything or did anything."

"Remembered what?"

With its lights flashing, a police car raced into the park and down the road. The crowd surged out of the way.

Cheryl pushed forward to meet the young trooper who stepped out of the car. "They're in the woods. My husband and this man's wife. She tried to kill him, and he—" Another sob. "He's dangerous."

The policeman stared at her. An illicit relationship gotten out of hand? For this they needed the police?

"Go find them!" Cheryl screamed. The trooper reached into his car for a lantern and headed into the woods. Cheryl started after him.

"You'd better keep out of the way," Brian told her.

She pounded her face with her hands, digging in her fingernails. "I don't know what to do!" she cried.

"Leonard can take care of himself," he told her angrily. "It's Theresa I'm worried about."

192

"You said she wanted to kill him."

"And you know who's going to kill who. Now what were you saying about Leonard?"

"About that thing that happened to Theresa."

"Tell me."

"I thought you knew."

"Tell me."

"About the boys. In high school. And the sand pit."

"My God," he breathed. "It wasn't a dream."

"He thought she didn't remember, because—"

"She didn't, except as a nightmare. She wanted to kill him because she thought he killed Patty."

"But he thought she did, because of him." Cheryl's fists beat the air. "I don't know what to do."

Bonnie came up to her and tugged at her coat.

"Go back!" shrieked Cheryl.

"Mark went out and I want to know what's happening."

Cheryl raised her hand, then let it drop. "I'm just like him," she wept. "Bonnie." She reached out for her child, but Bonnie was gone.

Theresa caught the flash of a light. They were looking for her. She didn't know who they were, or where she was, or why. Only that Leonard was here and he would kill her. He knew where she was now. He had heard her when she tried to move away from the tree.

"Hold it right there, bitch," he said.

She shrank away from him. *Michael,* she thought, not daring to speak aloud. *Michael, help me!*

Leonard's foot struck her shoe.

Michael!

Michael was angry. She had blamed him for everything. But he had gotten her into this. He had attacked Leonard, and she was starting to remember what Leonard had done.

He stepped back.

"Damn bitch," said Leonard's voice.

"Sure," said Michael. "It's all her fault, right?"

He saw a shadow rise up and lunge at him. Quickly he dodged to one side. His fist caught Leonard in the stomach.

He heard the air rush out. Leonard groaned.

"How would you like to be buried in sand?" Michael said. "How would you like to be gang-raped by a bunch of kids twice your size? How would you like it to happen to your daughter? That's how old she was. And how innocent."

The shadow moved again and he punched again. This time he struck a hard shoulder. He felt it give under his knuckles as Leonard spun.

A light flickered through the woods. Michael could see the direction it was coming in, and darted out of the way. A beam showed Leonard slumped against a tree. He shook his head, squinting in the light, and pulled himself upright.

"Okay, mister," said the policeman, "you want to come with me? Your wife is waiting for you."

Laughing silently, Michael glided away through the darkness. He knew where the path was. He knew these woods. They were his territory, never Theresa's. He followed the path until he reached an overgrown dirt road that ran out to the highway.

Then he heard her voice.

"Come home with me, Michael."

He stopped and listened. Was she giving him orders? That was not the Theresa he knew.

"Why should I?" he asked. "You tried to kill me. And now I'm going to live my own life."

He could barely hear her whisper. "You can't. We have to work out something together. I want to be both of us."

"I want to be me."

"I want to be you, too. You're strong and wonderful, and I'm not."

"I'm a man."

"Women can be strong and wonderful, too. I'm only half a person, Michael."

194

"You're a limp dishrag," he scoffed. "And you tried to kill me."

"Because I thought you killed Patty."

"And now?"

"You didn't, Michael, I know you didn't. You were only trying to find out who did."

Her voice was soft and seductive. He didn't want to be seduced, not by her.

"You won't die," she promised, "because you're me. You're part of me."

He still wasn't sure. "You have the body," he said.

"And you have the memory. That's part of a person, too."

He could have gone on by himself, gone away somewhere and had a life, but there were practical considerations. There were problems such as not having any money on him, and the fact that Brian and maybe even the police would be looking for him.

Or rather, they would be looking for Theresa. And that brought up what was likely the most serious problem of all.

He walked along the highway until he reached the park entrance. Then he slipped down the center road and made his way home unseen.

25

Brian found her at home in the kitchen, opening a package of fish sticks.

"Did you eat?" she asked.

"My God, how did you get here?"

"What do you mean?"

"They were looking for you in the woods. I thought he was going to kill you."

"In the woods? What are you talking about?"

"Weren't you there? Cheryl said you and Freaney were fighting and she saw you go into the woods."

She looked at him blankly. Not even mystified. He was hardly surprised. The whole story the Freaneys had told was damned crazy.

He took her hand. "Are you all right now?"

"What do you mean 'now'? Of course I'm all right."

"You were pretty upset earlier. And you ran away from me when I was trying to call the doctor."

"That's because you were treating me like an invalid. I hate that."

"I was worried about you."

"I know."

She withdrew her hand. She was beginning to feel the blows Michael had given to Leonard, but Brian mustn't know about that.

196

He said, "Cheryl told me what happened that time."

"What do you mean?"

"About Leonard. When you were little. The dream you had."

"How did she know?"

"He told her last night. He thought you were trying to get back at him. He thought that explained the poison."

"Oh. Really."

So Leonard wasn't the killer after all. She didn't know who it was, but at least it wasn't Michael.

"What happened to Leonard?" she asked.

"The police have him now. They wanted to talk to him."

"About what?"

"About what happened tonight. He swears you attacked him, but I don't believe it. And when they found him, he smelled of alcohol."

She did not reply. Brian said, "It won't be the first time he's been wrong."

"What do you mean?"

"I think Cheryl will have a lot to say to them. She's all in a sweat over that thing that happened to you."

Theresa stood leaning against the refrigerator, her eyes cast down. Remembering. She seemed thoughtful and sad, not angry. That was so like her. He couldn't believe she would have gone after Leonard, in spite of what he claimed, and in spite of her announcement that she was going to kill him. Probably the Freaneys had just imagined it was she, because of their own guilt feelings.

He turned to look out of the window. All the Freaneys' lights were on and two police cars were parked in front. He didn't know what the police were going to learn. He would leave it to them. If it hadn't been for Patty and those others, he might have backed Mark all the way, because he certainly understood what had driven him.

But Patty was dead. Murdered. He could think of Leonard as the killer. Leonard killed souls, if not bodies, but Mark had

197

done the deed. He could almost hear Mark telling them, "You thought I was so dumb."

Yes, Mark had done it, probably hoping to kill his father and maybe his mother, too, but at the same time he must have wanted to prove that he wasn't the incompetent weasel they always said he was. Poor kid. Brian's bitterness, mingled with compassion, nearly choked him. A really bright kid, but his parents ridiculed and belittled him, beat him down, because they couldn't understand him. They felt threatened by their son because he was brighter than they, and they were insecure. If they had treated him right, he might have done them proud.

Instead, he had killed six people. Six people, with cyanide probably stolen from Boyd Wentz's secret supply. Boyd must have bragged to Mark that he had the stuff. Brian could imagine the rapport between those two brilliant but thwarted minds. He could imagine Mark building on his plot, his cover-up, bicycling into Pine Glen, haunting the Valley Center markets during his lunch hour from the Middle School there. True to Lou Fiedler's description, he was a loner, so no one had accompanied him, no one had missed him, no one ever questioned what he was doing.

Killing and killing, when what he really wanted was to free himself from his father. To be free to be himself, and now he never would be.

Let the police find out, if they could. Brian would never say anything to anyone.

26

"Didn't you ever have a time," asked the doctor, "when things got so terrible you just wished you didn't have to be there any more? That you could escape out of the life you were living, or escape into another?"

Brian guessed he had, briefly, especially in Vietnam. But by and large, his life had been a piece of cake compared with Theresa's.

"Is that what happened?" he asked. "She escaped into being somebody else?"

"Multiple personality is a very rare disorder," the doctor explained, "but when it happens, it's usually a result of some trauma that the person simply can't handle. The alternate personality, or personalities, are suppressed aspects of himself. Maybe the one that comes out at a given time is better able to cope with that situation, or take the pain of the situation and then himself disappear."

"You mean that other personality is really part of her? But it's a man."

"Probably Theresa sees women as passive victims. Then the coping personality, the one that's able to show all the aggressiveness she can't show, might be in the form of a man. We all have both male and female aspects to ourselves. When Theresa and Michael are finally fused into one person, I think you'll find a true woman in every glorious sense of the word."

"Will it take long?"

"That's hard to say. It depends on how things go. She seems very positive about it, so I have hopes of its moving right along. Why, you weren't planning to go anywhere, were you?"

"No, we like it here in Arizona. It's what we both need. A new start. Theresa suggested it after our little girl died. She wanted to go away someplace where nobody knew us. And we couldn't stay there, with the Freaneys living right across from us."

"I certainly hope that family gets help," said the doctor.

"They need it. But whatever they get, it's going to be too late for a lot of things."

"You're thinking of your daughter."

"Will I ever stop?"

"Probably not, but I can help you deal with the bitterness."

"Maybe that's what I need. I wanted to get my hands on the killer, and when I found out who it was, I couldn't do anything."

"If you could have, do you think it would have made you feel better?"

"I don't know," said Brian. "I really don't know."

200